MW01256316

Best.

Mf
Cossock

Max Cossack

BLESSED WITH ALL THIS LIFE

Copyright © 2022 Max Cossack

All Rights Reserved

ISBN: 978-1-7370167-6-2

All rights are reserved under International and Pan-American copyright conventions. Without written permission of the author no part of this book may be reproduced, transmitted, or down-loaded by any means electronic or mechanical, including but not limited to photocopying, recording, down-loading, or reverse engineering, nor may it be stored or otherwise introduced into any information storage and retrieval system by any means now known or hereafter invented.

This is a work of fiction. Names of characters, businesses or places, events or incidents, are the products of the author's imagination and are fictitious and not to be construed as real. Any resemblance to actual persons or organizations living or dead or actual events is purely coincidental.

Previous novels by Max Cossack in *The Wilder Bunch* series, in chronological order:

1. *Khaybar, Minnesota*
2. *Zarah's Fire*
3. *Simple Grifts: A Comedy of Social Justice*
4. *Low Tech Killers*
5. *Where There Is No Man*
6. *Social Credit: A Comic Novel of Globalist Proportions*

Other books published by VWAM include these by Susan Vass:
Ammo Grrrll Hits The Target (Volume 1)
Ammo Grrrll Aims True (Volume 2)
Ammo Grrrll Returns Fire (Volume 3)
Ammo Grrrll Is Home On The Range (Volume 4)
Ammo Grrrll Is A Straight Shooter (Volume 5)
Ammo Grrrll Reloads (Volume 6)
Ammo Grrrll Gets (a) Shot (Volume 7)

To the Memory of Nadezhda Mandelstam,
May her memory be a blessing
(זכרונה לברכה)

EPIGRAPHICA

טו עֲצַבֵּי הַגּוֹיִם, כֶּסֶף וְזָהָב ;מַעֲשֵׂה, יְדֵי אָדָם

טז פֶּה-לָהֶם, וְלֹא יְדַבֵּרוּ ;עֵינַיִם לָהֶם, וְלֹא יִרְאוּ

יז אָזְנַיִם לָהֶם, וְלֹא יַאֲזִינוּ ;אַף, אֵין-יֶשׁ-רוּחַ בְּפִיהֶם

יח כְּמוֹהֶם, יִהְיוּ עֹשֵׂיהֶם--כֹּל אֲשֶׁר-בֹּטֵחַ בָּהֶ

15 The idols of the nations are silver and gold, the work of
men's hands.
16 They have mouths, but they do not speak; they have eyes,
but they do not see;
17 They have ears, but they do not hear, nor is there any
breath in their mouths.
18 Those who make them will become like them, as will those
who trust in them.

Psalm 135

"Full many a flow'r is born to blush unseen,
And waste its sweetness on the desert air."
Thomas Gray, *Elegy Written In A Country Churchyard*

"Crooked never stops."
Mattie Wilder

"Play what you hear, not what you know."
Henry Wadsworth

BOOK 1:

THEN

1 Henry Wadsworth

Hack was 17 the first time he heard Henry Wadsworth play piano.

It was at a club on Chicago's North Side. Hack had come to Chicago for college, no definite idea what he was going to study, but thrilled to be out of the Minnesota boonies, exploring one of the great cities of the world.

On the first Tuesday night of that first college October, Hack and two random freshman dorm-mates were strolling Chicago's fabled Clark Street, enjoying the glare of the lights and the mindless bustle and chatter of the crowd.

They were looking for adventure, or at least a way to get their hands on some liquor, maybe from one of the many drunks who stationed themselves outside liquor stores and proxy-bought for the underaged in exchange for booze of their own.

The three strolled past a dark brick storefront to a concrete arch. Someone had scotch-taped on the arch a white sheet of notebook paper which fluttered in the cool autumn breeze. They had inked on the sheet in neat black letters:

Henry Wadsworth Tonight

In the shadows below the arch, three concrete steps led down to a gray steel door. Reflections from the headlights of passing cars flickered in the door's brass handle.

If a bar with a relaxed attitude lay just the other side of that door, they might get some beer.

Hack walked down the steps and his buddies followed. They stopped just outside the door. The three exchanged glances. Hack sucked it up and grabbed the handle and pulled the door open.

They stepped into a thirty-by-thirty space crammed with empty tables and chairs. In the dark corner on their right a trio was playing loud music. The pianist sat facing away, his round back hunched over the keyboard of a five-foot grand piano whose keys phosphoresced white in the gloom. A drummer sat in the corner, trapped behind the piano. The upright bass player had somehow squeezed both his narrow self and his instrument into the tight space between piano and drums.

Both sidemen wore old-fashioned fedoras down low over their faces.

This was no cocktail music. It was loud as electric blues or heavy metal, although the cascading notes rang pure and true, with no distortion.

Hack and his buddies threaded their way among the many empty tables. Hack chose a table as far from the boisterous waves of sound as he could get.

Even there, the sound washed over and around and through Hack. He had no idea what the sound meant or if it meant anything at all. It was obvious the trio intended the sound as music, but this was a music as alien to Hack as the exotic Chicago streets and the exotic Chicago people prowling them.

On the off chance the waitress wouldn't card them, the boys ordered beer. They had to settle for soft drinks.

On the other hand, she didn't throw them out, which seemed sufficient miracle at the time. Maybe that was because they were her only three customers.

Stooped over his piano keyboard, his back to his audience, the pianist never glanced back, except sometimes between tunes, when he did terse crowd patter, turning his head halfway towards the room and muttering out of the side of his mouth something like, "Now, *In Walked Bud.*"

Then they played what must be *In Walked Bud*, which to Hack sounded a lot like the old Irving Berlin song *Blue Skies*.

It was the only song the entire night Hack thought he recognized.

Sometimes the pianist's entire patter amounted to, "Now we're going to play another tune." Then the trio played another tune.

Song names didn't matter. Hack had never heard any of them before.

Though Hack considered himself a musician, he understood almost nothing of this music. There was never the comforting simplicity of a pop melody. The music seemed as complex as classical music.

But no matter how hard Hack concentrated, he never tracked anything like the repeated theme of a classical composition, always recognizable no matter how ingenious or convoluted the variations through which a Bach or a Beethoven or a Brahms worked it, the way those old-time guys had of wringing out of a few simple notes every drop of melodic and harmonic possibility.

After the first few minutes, Hack gave up trying to track any ideas in the music. He sipped his root beer and let the sound wash over him. Maybe he'd figure it out later.

After all, he hadn't understood Haydn or Mozart either when he first heard their pieces as a twelve-year-old. His Ojibwa City piano teacher Ms. Lager ordered him to learn to play them, so he did. Only after playing them for a month or two did he begin to understand them. Until then, he was playing notes he read off pages of sheet music.

To Hack's American ears, learning European classical music was like learning a foreign language. If you wanted to understand it, you had to learn to speak it at least a little.

No matter what Hack did or didn't understand, the pianist's music fascinated him. Hack had never heard such unstudied and spontaneous piano playing.

But that wasn't right either. The pianist wasn't making music; it was more like the music just came out of him, often

3

in a mad torrent, but every so often in a sweet soft murmur, a hushed tender language Hack could imagine himself speaking to a girl in his bed, should he ever convince a girl to climb into bed with him.

The bassist and drummer weren't much older than Hack. They paid no attention to the room. They focused on the pianist and played with grim determination, as if they had to work even harder than Hack, which he realized they did, since they actually had to play.

From time to time a customer or two wandered in and had a drink or two and shook his head and left.

Soon, Hack's two buddies grew bored with the scene and wandered out to go find liquor, or at least "some decent music."

As it happened, Hack never hung with them again. College was like that, especially that freshman year.

Hack stayed until closing. After the trio's final tune, his back still to the room, the pianist stood and gently closed the piano fallboard over the keys. The waitress walked over and handed him a few bills. He split the cash with his two bandmates, who packed up and took off.

Hack got up his nerve and crossed the thirty feet to the pianist and said, "That's amazing music."

The pianist turned and blinked. Hack realized for the first time he was a black man. He was stocky, hardly taller than Hack's five-foot-six, but thicker. He cropped his hair short. His dark suit looked out of date—the collars were too wide—but it was spotless and pressed neat and flat against his solid chest.

A bright orange pocket square poked up from his front suit pocket. The way his orange square and orange bow tie clashed with his pink dress shirt reminded Hack of the way the chords he played so often clashed with each other.

He peered at Hack with evident curiosity, as if Hack were an unaccountable new species. He mumbled, "Thank you."

4

Hack asked, "Do you give lessons?"

The pianist stepped a few inches back from Hack. In simultaneous counter motion, he tilted his head forward and peered closer. He seemed to squint at this odd creature before him. He said, "Depends."

"I'll pay."

"That helps," the pianist said.

2 An Audition

Hack didn't sleep Tuesday night until after 5 AM. He lay in darkness on his back on his dorm room bed, staring upwards, while Henry Wadsworth's exotic riffs and spectacular runs replayed in his mind.

The runs and riffs made no sense to Hack. Why? Because they made no sense? Or was it Hack's failure, some lack in himself which rendered him unable to identify the sense which must be there?

After all, if there was no sense in their music, why had Wadsworth and his two sidemen attacked its creation with so much technical competence and earnest authority?

Who was wrong? Hack or them?

Hack's world had been an orderly place, monotonous even, in particular his world of tiny Ojibwa City, a backwoods village on the edge of the jackpine Minnesota wilderness, where he knew everybody and everybody knew him, where friendships and expectations were settled, where everybody knew what music was, just the way they knew what baseball was, and for Hack's family and some of his neighbors, the soybeans were high and the living was easy.

Wednesday morning Hack called the number Mr. Wadsworth had given him.

The next morning, they were in Mr. Wadsworth's apartment off Clark Street, a few blocks from the club. Hack was sitting on the piano stool in front of Henry's old black upright.

It was one of those old-fashioned revolving piano stools, the kind whose seat the player could twirl up or down to a comfortable height. Hack had needed to twirl it up only one spin. It seemed Mr. Wadsworth and he were about the same height, at least sitting down.

Mr. Wadsworth had stationed himself to Hack's right on a wooden chair he'd carried in from the kitchen and unfolded.

Mr. Wadsworth said to Hack, "Play something."

Hack hated playing piano for strangers. Piano was something you did all alone with no one around. You didn't need anyone else.

With just your piano, you could create your own band or even orchestra once you figured out how.

Hack had played in public only that one scary time in Junior High. It wasn't just fear, although the notion of playing in public did make his knees quake. It was more that music was a private matter, like religion or sex, none of anyone else's business.

Hack's playing was his practicing, and his practicing was his playing, and both happened only at home.

Almost the only people who'd ever heard Hack play were his mother and father, and once by accident his buddy Gus, who'd biked into town from his old white farmhouse on the edge of the jackpines. They'd planned to head out together to wander around in the woods near town.

Gus sat waiting for Hack outside on the front stoop until Hack finished. When Hack finished his practicing and came out, neither he nor Gus said anything about it.

After some prodigious effort at a Chopin Waltz, Hack's mother would say, "That sounds nice," or "Please don't stop," and smile.

His dad never commented on Hack's playing. But once in a while he'd say, "You should listen to this," and play a recording for Hack, usually somebody Hack had never heard, like Frank Zappa or Pat Metheny or some gypsy band from Spain. His dad had weird tastes in everything, maybe from having been overseas so much.

After which Hack nodded in appreciation and said, "That's good," and rarely listened to that record again until much later, after his dad passed, although the music his dad showed him

7

lurked somewhere inside, poised to come out at surprising times.

From this behavior and no other, Hack got the idea his father approved of his pounding on the piano keys every evening after school and baseball.

Hack had never in his life tried out for anything. He never wanted to. Now, asking Mr. Wadsworth for lessons, Hack argued to himself that the man's request for an audition was reasonable. How else could a teacher judge what he needed to teach?

Just this one time.

Hack lifted and relaxed his shoulders and dropped them. He exhaled until it felt like he'd emptied his lungs, then drew in a deep breath. He ran his fingertips up and down over the keys the way Ms. Lager had taught him, searching for a sense of this particular piano's touch, whether stiff or easy.

He put his hands back in his lap and looked down at them and made a mental effort to suppress the trembling. You can't play piano with shaking hands.

Hack chose the piece he thought he played best. The adrenaline rush spooked him into starting it too fast. He caught himself and slowed down too far. Now he was making a mess of the tempo. Frustrated, he nevertheless played through to the bitter end. Finished, he stared down at the keys and waited for the inevitable negative judgment.

"Very beautifully played," Mr. Wadsworth said. "Maybe as well as anyone I ever heard play *Claire De Lune*. It's a piece from Debussy's *Suite Bergamesque*. But of course, you know that."

No, Hack didn't know that. It was just a six-page sheaf of sheet music Ms. Lager had plunked in front of him on a music stand and asked him to start playing. He did know the piece was strange, though, nothing like the Bach and Beethoven and Chopin she'd previously assigned him. But he'd never thought about what made it strange or why that should be.

Mr. Wadsworth went on, "Of course, when he wrote this, Debussy was about to make a revolution in music. As in this piece. No obvious thematic development from beginning to middle to end, like with all those German composers in their sonata-form concertos and symphonies. What the French called 'impressionism', although Debussy hated that word. He was more about creating a mood or a feeling or an atmosphere than conveying any impression of anything. But impressionism was big in French art at the time, and the term stuck."

"Impressionism" and "sonata-form" and "thematic development" became the first of the hundreds of Wadsworth words and phrases Hack didn't recognize and had to go look up in the college library.

Mr. Wadsworth asked, "You know the poem?"

There was a poem?

Mr. Wadsworth registered Hack's blank expression. "Debussy got his idea from a poem by the French poet Verlaine. *Claire De Lune.* You should check it out. You don't happen to know any French, do you?"

"No," Hack admitted. "Just a little Spanish from high school."

Mr. Wadsworth stared off into space and recited a few lines of what must have been French. Mr. Wadsworth's voice was soft, but commanding, like he meant what he said, whatever it was.

Mr. Wadsworth turned back to Hack and asked, "Did you notice there's no root notes played in the bass in the beginning?"

"Not really," Hack admitted. Root notes?

"Just D-flat chords but without the root D-flats themselves," Mr. Wadsworth explained.

Hack pictured the sheet music. Mr. Wadsworth was right, of course. No low D-flats at the very beginning. Why? Were those the "root notes"?

"Mr. Wadsworth," Hack began.

"Call me Henry," Henry said.

"Henry," Hack said. "I don't know anything you're talking about."

Henry smiled. It was a big broad smile. "You don't know how happy I am to hear that," he said. "You're sort of an empty slate, aren't you?"

Was that true? Before he heard Henry play, Hack had an idea he might be pretty good, at least comparing himself to recordings and people he heard around his little town.

"Except one very important thing," Henry said. "I mean, I don't know who taught you—"

"Ms. Lager back in Ojibwa City."

"Ojibwa City? What's that?"

"It's a tiny Minnesota town, on the edge of the jackpines. You never heard of it."

Henry asked, "Near Minneapolis? I've played there."

"About an hour-and-a-half away."

"And who's this Ms. Lager? Where'd she come from?"

Hack had no answer. Ms. Lager was just Ms. Lager, the local piano teacher. You never wondered where adults came from. He shrugged.

"You were lucky to have her, wherever she came from," Henry said. "You've got the right technique. You even sit right, and this Ms. Lager taught you how to use your legs, which most pianists never even heard about, and you're listening to what you're playing while you play. You're paying attention. I can tell. That's a great foundation."

"Thank you."

"Don't thank me too soon, Nate," Henry said. "You got work to do."

3 Sessions In Wadsworth

It was Hack's second lesson. At their first lesson, Henry had showed him a blues chord progression. Hack took his first shot at playing the blues for Henry, who asked, "Nate, what's all that shaking and moving?"

Henry always called him "Nate." Like his mom. Even his dad had started calling him "Hack" after the high school baseball nickname landed and stuck.

Hack asked, "What do you mean?"

"You're shaking your head and waving yourself around, like something's stuck up your ass and you got to shake yourself loose."

"Showmanship?"

"Showmanship?" Henry echoed. "You want people to watch or to listen?"

"It helps me get into the feeling of what I'm playing."

"Your choice," Henry said. "I'm not going to tell you what to do with your body. But you don't need all that moving and shaking. If you're inside the music and it's inside you, and you play right, the feeling will come out on its own without any showmanship or whatever you call it. Try focusing on the music and not on yourself and see what happens. You might play better."

Hack scrapped the showmanship and of course Henry was right. And as the music Henry taught him challenged Hack more and more, Hack had all he could do just to get the right notes out at the right time. The less he focused on watching himself play and the more he focused on the music itself, the better the sounds coming out of his piano.

The next session—Henry insisted they call their times together "sessions" rather than lessons—after another try at some blues, Henry asked, "Have you met Mr. Metronome?"

"Sure," Hack said. "Ms. Lager showed me. It clicks out the beat at any tempo you want."

"Have you thought about using it?"

"You mean, while I play?" Hack asked.

"While you practice."

"Ms. Lager told me it's handy for setting a tempo, but I should turn it off as soon as I start to play."

"Why's that?"

"She said it will make you lose the feeling in the music and play like a machine instead of a human being."

"That's true for the music Ms. Lager taught you, like Chopin or those other European masters," Henry admitted. "The rhythmic conception is different in that music. But in our American music you got to stick with the beat. Even if you decide to play off the beat, you still got to know where it is."

Hack asked, "I'm not on the beat?"

"I'll let Mr. Metronome teach you that," Henry said. "He never lies. He just speaks the awful truth. From now on, practice with Mr. Metronome ticking away. He'll let you know when you get the time or the rhythm wrong."

"You mean when I'm playing a blues like this one?"

"For the time being, everything," Henry said. "Every exercise, every drill, every tune."

That afternoon Hack went down to a local music store and spent thirty precious dollars on a palm-sized electronic metronome.

He took it back to the piano in his dorm room lounge and turned it on. He set it to a tempo of 90 beeps per minute. Its beeps were weak and timid, as if it were nervous about interrupting. It was barely loud enough to hear over his piano. He put in his shirt pocket to bring it closer to his ears, but that helped only a little. Then he noticed the little headphone jack and plugged headphones into it.

With the metronome chirping in his ears, he started a simple left hand barrelhouse riff. Ten seconds in, the beep fell behind. He'd raced ahead. He started again. This time, he fell behind.

A half hour in, he was managing to play at roughly the same tempo as the nasty little bastard. But he wasn't playing the beat, he was only approximating its beat, sometimes ahead, sometime behind, which wasn't the same thing at all.

For days, then weeks, even months, so it went, with everything he practiced or played.

He tried tapping his foot along with the metronome, which for some reason helped, as if getting his body into the beat helped him feel it and play it.

Some musicians seemed to be able to keep a solid beat right out of the chute, but Hack wasn't one of them. No point in jealousy. Hack had his own advantages, including a piano technique he soon learned few of his college classmates could match, which Henry called "chops."

It was just that the chops were meaningless without also what Henry called a "sense of time."

As Hack worked and the months rolled by, Henry began issuing occasional compliments, like "pretty decent," or "not so bad," or "I'm beginning to hear a difference," and pushed Hack to stick with it, which he did.

After a few months, Hack's developing sense of time and knowledge of scales and chords propelled him into his snob phase. He couldn't shut up about what he was learning.

The rhythmic limitations of other musicians began to annoy. He couldn't help noticing which fellow students couldn't stick to the starting tempo, which coffeehouse guitarists strummed clatter instead of rhythm, which rock drummers didn't rock.

At the peak of Hack's snob phase, there came a time when Hack sat with a girl in a coffee house and wrecked his feeble chances with her by pointing out that the folkie guitar player had no sense of time and that his "blues" were a pastel turquoise at best.

From her negative reaction, he learned to keep his mouth shut, but he found himself beaming frustrated private thoughts at musicians, like *find the beat, or change up the chords a little*, or *just try a different riff for once*, or *do something or anything new or at least different from what I've already heard a thousand times.*

Late that first year, Henry took Hack's place on the bench and showed him how to play a left-hand Latin rhythm in the bass to go with a righthand melody. Henry added, "This will come in handy when there's no bass player on your gig."

A gig? Hack had never been on a gig. He'd never imagined a gig. "Gig" was a word as new and alien to him as Henry's way of thinking about music.

Henry said, "Are you listening to what I'm saying?"

Hack caught himself. "Sure," he said. "It's a lefthand part for a bossa nova. To play on a gig. When there's no bass player. On the gig. If such an event should ever occur."

4 The Beehive

On the edge of the campus stood a rotting three-story brick building with two dozen miniscule rooms, each barely big enough to contain an old upright piano and its routinely rickety bench. Students called it "The Beehive." Hack began to practice in the Beehive hours per day.

He mentioned the Beehive to Henry at a session.

"That's an opportunity for you," Henry said from his usual place on his wooden folding chair. "Not everyone has easy access to a piano. I went years without my own. I had to sneak into local churches."

"But they're all out of tune," Hack said.

Henry asked, "Every single one?"

"Yes."

"They never tune them at all?"

Hack shook his head. "Maybe. But not very well."

"How are you so sure?"

"I can hear it."

"Close your eyes," Henry said.

Hack closed his eyes.

Henry hit a single a single piano key. "What's this note?"

"B Flat."

Another key. "And this?"

"G sharp."

Instead of playing the next note, Henry hummed it.

Hack opened his eyes. "That's an F."

"Did you know you have perfect pitch?"

"I never thought about it," Hack said. "Doesn't everyone recognize the notes they hear?"

"No," Henry said. "They don't. Some don't even after you tell them. I mean, even other musicians. Or they can't even recognize intervals, like the major-third jump from a C to an E."

Now Henry had to explain what an interval was—the distance in half steps between two notes.

Strange. Ms. Lager never mentioned perfect pitch, but at least this time Henry was talking about something Hack had heard of. He had an idea what perfect pitch was.

Might come in handy. Maybe even on a gig.

Henry stood and left the room. A moment later he came back with a foot-long bag of worn brown leather. A strap with big buckles was wrapped tight around it. Henry said, "I've got three. You can have this old one."

"What is it?"

"A piano tuning kit." Henry handed Hack the bag.

Hack hefted the bag and laid it on his lap. He unbuckled the strap and unrolled the bag. Inside he found a lever about twelve inches long. The lever had a six-inch wood handle and chrome-plated shaft with a square metal tip.

"Tuning lever," Henry explained. "You use it to tighten and loosen the piano strings. That's how you raise and lower their pitch to get the piano in tune."

"What are these?" Hack pointed to a few black rubber wedges in the open bag on his lap. Some were about three inches long. Some were a bit longer.

"Figure that part yourself," Henry said. "And this is a tuning fork." Henry took the metal pronged tool from the open bag in Hack's lap and laid it on a nearby table. "I'll keep this and save it for someone who needs it."

"Like another student?"

"You're my only student, Nate."

How could that be?

Hack asked, "How do I use this?"

"You'll come up with something," Henry said.

As a teacher, Henry had his own individual ways. One of his most irritating was to force Hack to puzzle things out on his own, whether it was the fingering he needed to play a tough keyboard passage, or the logic behind a complicated chord progression, or as in this case, tuning a piano.

He'd say, "I had to figure that out for myself. So can you. That's the best way to learn anyway. What you figure out for yourself sticks with you."

Henry kept telling Hack to figure things out until Hack gave up asking the simpler questions and began to operate with the presumption he'd have to learn almost every answer on his own.

Hack went back to the school library and found a book on piano tuning. He took the book and his new toolkit to the Beehive and from then on tuned every piano before he played it. His first try took him two hours, but over time he got faster and more efficient, until he could tune even the sourest offender in a few minutes.

It turned out a lot of Beehive pianos needed more than tuning. An acoustic piano is a complicated and fragile mechanism. Fingers stroke keys, which through complicated mechanisms trigger hammers, which then hit strings hung in a tension so extreme that the instrument requires an iron frame just to stay intact.

Many Beehive pianos were missing parts. Sometimes the parts they did have were damaged or broken. Hack wound up doing more research in the library and more tinkering on broken instruments in the Beehive, until he was sure he could have qualified as a piano repairman.

The problem was money. After paying for tuition, books, food, sessions and an occasional pizza or beer, Hack had none to spare.

The woman in charge of the Beehive was Mrs. Simpson. He found himself nagging Mrs. Simpson into buying clutches of new strings and hammers and keys and other parts. She didn't seem to mind. Quite the opposite; she indulged him.

Eventually, he figured out that he was doing her a favor by repairing all her pianos. His work was a free supplement to her meager budget.

Looking back later, Hack remembered very little about his dark years in the Beehive. Everyone called the little piano rooms "cells," like the cells medieval monks wrote and fasted in, poorly lit and never heated or air conditioned.

A better comparison for the Beehive might have been to a low-security self-imprisonment. Hack voluntarily locked himself away in the cells. In them, he practiced scales and drills and everything Henry told him without any leniency towards himself.

Even 17 or 18 or 19 was late in life to learn a musical instrument; he couldn't afford to waste any more time. He'd wasted too much already.

He was a thief of his own time, now dedicated to paying it back.

5 *Listening*

Hack had played only alone on his home piano, the ancient family upright fitted into a small side space off the living room. He wasn't sure where it came from, but he started picking out small tunes on it when he was six years old, long before he started his lessons with Ms. Lager at twelve.

The first time Hack tried to play with a bass player he met in college jazz class, the bass player let Hack call the first tune. Hack picked the Charlie Parker tune "Scrapple from the Apple," a tune he'd messed with from a book of tunes called *The Real Book*.

The two didn't make it through fifteen seconds together, and Hack was the reason.

"Train wreck", the bass player, a senior, said. "But let's try again." They did, then again at half speed, and this time Hack lasted thirty seconds before they gave up. The bass player didn't complain. He just shrugged and patted Hack on the shoulder and loaded up his bass and left.

Next session with Henry, Hack complained, "I got lost right out of the chute. I had no idea what he was playing or where he was in the tune."

"You have to listen."

"I listen. You said so the first time you heard me play."

"Not just to yourself," Henry said. "To everyone else too."

"All at the same time?"

"All at the same time," Henry said. "And it doesn't matter If there's just two of you or you're on a nine-foot grand with the Symphony."

"Wait," Hack said. "Let me guess. I'll figure it out for myself."

"Yes, you will," Henry said. "But only from doing it. One suggestion: try playing along with recordings. There are play-along recordings where they take out the piano part, like karaoke for piano. I bet you'll find some in that big college library of yours. Play along with those."

"Okay."

"They got a jazz big band at your college?"

"Yes."

"They got a college orchestra?"

"I think so."

"When you think you're ready, join both."

Sophomore year, Hack decided he was ready. Even though he felt he blew the auditions, the competition was weak, and Hack made it into both.

That's when Hack learned he had not only to listen, but to look. In the orchestra, he had to watch the conductor. In the big band, he had to keep his eye on the bandleader. In the small jazz and rock groups he began to play with, he had to make eye contact with all the others. All this while keeping his eyes on the piano keys—he wasn't Ray Charles, after all, he had to see the keys.

This was when terror entered Hack's musical life.

On the high school baseball field, mild cases of nerves had hit him from time to time, getting the signal to steal second base, or at the plate in the bottom of the ninth of a tie game.

But those annoyances never kept him from functioning. They triggered the mild rush of adrenaline which made him faster and stronger and smarter.

Piano nerves were different. Piano nerves didn't annoy, they attacked. They savaged him with merciless broadsides which left him confused, disoriented, and sometimes terrified.

Familiarity got Hack over his fear of playing for Henry, even though Henry was the most astute and the toughest critic Hack could ever meet.

It was playing among strangers Hack feared. Fear made it hard to breathe. Fear distracted, taking his mind off the path of the music Hack in which needed to immerse. Fear made his hands shake, and you can't play piano with shaking hands.

The fear wasn't so much a fear of embarrassment, although Hack felt the typical human concern not to look a fool.

Hack feared the clam. The clam isn't just the booboo typical in any challenging physical effort. After he made a few thousand of them, Hack came to feel an occasional wrong note in music no worse than a dropped foul popup or a muffed grounder in baseball. Yeah, it was bad, but everybody did it sooner or later. It happens. Hack got to the point where he almost laughed.

People are used to the perfection of recordings. But recordings are often lies. No one plays or sings perfect music all the time. In the studio, instrumentalists replay parts they messed up. Singers sing a song until they get it right. Engineers fix sour notes with autotuning software.

Clams happen live. No one can miss a clam. The clam makes everyone wince, not just the bandleader or conductor or your fellow musicians, but the audience as well.

The clam is no timid wimp of a mistake like a muffed note or a lost beat.

The clam is big and bold. The clam doesn't sneak into the song and whisper its presence like a little wussy-pants. The clam marches in and bellows "Here I am!"

Henry gave him a few tips. "When you play a clam, never show it in your face. Never apologize. And whatever you do, don't stop playing. Keep going. If you can do it without wrecking the song, play the mistake again, like you mean it, loud and strong. So maybe your clam turns the song from major to minor. If you can, go ahead and keep playing in minor. Follow your mistake —maybe it'll take you someplace good."

In the end, Hack overcame his terror in the most painful way possible: he hammered out every clam there was and survived.

At a college big band concert, he lost his place in a piece and played the same section twice while everyone else forged ahead without him—even the non-musicians in the crowd knew somebody was wrong, and they had to know the wrongest sounds were coming from his piano.

With the college orchestra, during the oboe solo in the slow and lovely second movement of a symphony, a single careless moment brought his big stupid elbow smashing down on the keyboard, shattering everyone's moment of enchantment.

This time, no doubt about it—two hundred people looked at Hack.

As Hack botched and bungled and blundered through piece after piece without the earth ever spiraling into the sun—not even once—his terror began to fade. The power of the clam abated. Clams continued to embarrass and irritate but no longer immobilized.

During that second year, according to Henry, most of what Hack played for him was "pretty decent,", but there was always a way to make it better.

Once Henry handed Hack a *Book of Scales and Patterns* and said, "Learn these."

When Hack thought he'd mastered the patterns and played a few for Henry, Henry said, "Now learn those in every key."

Followed a few months later by, "You've learned those riffs. Now make up your own."

Good things started to happen. For one college concert, a small trio had been selected from the big band, with Hack on piano. A student singer lost her way and started to sing the middle part of the song a second time—another train headed off the tracks. Hack heard her. He followed her and played the same wrong part she was singing. Without an instant's hesitation, the bass player followed Hack's lead. No one in the audience could know the singer's mistake.

For the first time, Hack felt like a real musician.

If no one heard it, it wasn't a clam, was it?

6 What Are You After?

"What are you after?" Henry asked Hack.

The session had just begun. Hack was poised on the piano stool, eager to show off what he'd just learned. Henry was sitting in his usual wooden chair, this time holding a can of beer in his right hand.

Hack hadn't seen him with a beer before. Henry didn't seem at all drunk, just relaxed, friendly, even avuncular.

"What do you mean?" Hack asked.

"I mean, why does music matter so much to you? I know you must be practicing. Every week I show you new things and the next week you show up and you've nailed them down."

What Hack was after was that he wasn't going to squander this once-in-a-lifetime chance. A master was giving him personal lessons in something—anything. Tony Gwynn was coaching Hack on hitting the curve ball. Ernest Hemingway was tutoring him on writing short stories.

This musician whose music Hack wondered at and still hadn't figured out was maybe an unrecognized genius, and he was devoting precious time to Hack, not just teaching him piano, but music in general, and Hack began to realize, matters beyond music.

Hack had no idea what all the sessions would amount to, or even if they would amount to anything, but he was going to grab his chance to hang out with this master.

Hack didn't say any of this to Henry. He said only, "I don't know," which was also true.

For two years Hack had devoted himself to one thing, and that was piano. He skimmed his required math and science and English textbooks. Even so, he rarely failed the courses. It was college time, and the grading was easy.

Hack scheduled his regular classes in the morning. He spent almost every afternoon through evening in the Beehive, emerging only a few times a day, eyes blinking at the glare of sunlight or snowdrift, to scarf a burger and a root beer and head back in.

The music he studied wasn't just Henry's. After talking it over with Henry, Hack decided to major in Music Composition, which at this school meant classical music. "Learn all you can," Henry told Hack. "They have a lot to teach you."

Learning to compose meant learning to play. Hack's primary Professor of Piano Performance was a shriveled Jewish woman from Hungary everyone called Miss Gabor at her insistence.

Miss Gabor rejected the "Ms." title with contempt. She wanted the world to know she was single and available.

Miss Gabor always looked exhausted, as if her ignorant students and their unrelenting sloth had worn her down to this sad spinster relic Hack saw before him. She paced the campus like an outraged ghost, glaring at every one of the thousands of under-brutalized Americans whose irritating good cheer flouted her well-earned misery.

Her default expression was a stern glare. She glared at everyone and always. For some reason she glared even harder at Hack, no matter how well he played his Chopin or Bach or Mozart, as if it were his fault these long-lost geniuses were dead—she seemed to suspect he'd shot and stabbed and poisoned them himself.

She always stank of cigarette smoke. But even through the nicotine-infused smog she radiated, she smelled out Hack's smallest errors of nuance as he fumbled his way through his assigned pieces.

Once in her office, after he played a Chopin nocturne for her—pretty well, he thought—she commented only, "You pedal like a peasant racing to market to dump his rotting chicken carcass on some naïve city slicker."

25

It took Hack a moment to realize she was talking about the sustain pedal under the piano, the pedal which lifts and holds the dampers off the strings and lets the notes ring out longer.

He asked, "What do you mean?"

She sighed, exhaling a gout of tar and nicotine vapor at him. "Too heavy! Too heavy!"

He suppressed his gag reflex and played the nocturne again, this time with a lighter foot, not so pedal-to-the-metal, and she gave him a barely mollified nod.

Once, after he gutted out a semi-decent performance of the nearly unplayable Liszt *Sonata in B Minor*—he spent his entire third year learning it—she did manage to puff out a whiff of almost-approval, and for one precious instant her clenched features unclenched.

Hack didn't mind. Hack had long been bored with the everyone-gets-a-trophy education system he'd grown up in and dozed through. It was fun to be challenged, even if the challenger stalked the campus in a cloak of gloom. Her acrid commentary kept him alert and attentive.

Hack made a private mind game of coming up with explanations for Miss Gabor. She'd lost her true love, maybe in the long-ago Hungarian Revolution against the Soviet Union—she looked old enough— or maybe that same heartless cad had betrayed her and broken her heart.

More likely, she'd started out as a musical prodigy, but fate relegated her to wasting her genius on spoiled American ignoramuses who couldn't imagine the hard work it takes to master any art beyond the easy mediocrity their enthusiastic teachers rewarded with counterfeit A's.

The wasted genius theory resonated with Hack's college experience. Someone like her would find American students irritating. He himself couldn't help noticing how arrogant so many were. How could anyone so ignorant be so arrogant?

Hack knew himself to be ignorant, His ignorance didn't bother him much, although the recognition of his ignorance drained him of arrogance. He figured ignorance was normal for a 19-year-old. If he wasn't ignorant, why study?

Hack correlated his classmates' taste for simple-minded music with their simple-minded approach to everything else, especially their own significance in the universe.

He supposed it had something to do with their upbringing. Most grew up in wealthy homes. They'd been told so often how wonderful they were that their instinctive youthful skepticism created doubt. This justifiable doubt led to insecurity. They compensated for their insecurity with bravado and false certainty on matters about which they knew nothing but a few slogans they picked up from their professors and their noisiest fellow students.

The frequent amalgam of political certainty and psychological insecurity startled and frightened. What was going to happen to these people when they left the campus? Or to the world they entered?

Later, Hack saw that they did just fine, even as they often inflicted their misery on others.

Except for Miss Gabor and a few oddballs, Hack's professors were irrelevant. After the first months, he tuned them out. The students and professors who waged their ceaseless political campaigns represented only mediocrity, unlike Henry and even Ms. Gabor, who offered excellence in something which mattered.

Although, when Henry asked Hack what he was after, and why it mattered, Hack had no answer.

7 *Going After It Hard*

Whatever Hack was after, Hack went after it hard.

Hack mentioned to Henry that he really liked the piano playing on a Sinatra ballad his flute player roommate Bennett had showed him. It was *One For My Baby (and One More For The Road)*.

Henry asked, "What do you like about it?"

Hack said, "The way he holds a rock-steady tempo, his great left hand, the bluesy feel he gives it, the whole thing."

"Who is he?" Henry asked.

"You don't know who Sinatra is?"

"I know who Sinatra is. Who is the pianist?"

"I don't know."

"Do you think maybe he played other things?" Henry asked. "Maybe on his own, without Sinatra?

"I don't know."

"Have you tried playing that song yourself?"

"Not really," Hack said. "I messed with it, that's all."

"If you like it, why not play it for real?"

"You mean, try to copy what he plays in the song?"

"You got ears," Henry said. "Good ones, too."

Hack copied Bennett's recording of the song onto his headphone music player. On the commercial recording, the orchestra drowned out much of the piano. But Bennett was a collector, and he also owned a rare recording of a rehearsal version featuring only Sinatra and the pianist. This pianist turned out to be someone Hack had never heard of, named Bill Miller, who ultimately died still on the road at age 91, by then playing not with the original Frank but with Frank Sinatra, Jr.

Hack took his music player to the Beehive and listened and tried his best to imitate Bill Miller. The longer Hack worked the harder it got. Miller wasn't just accompanying Sinatra, he was complementing him, telling his own story of lost love in parallel to Sinatra's. Like Sinatra singing in his Sinatra voice, Miller's piano sang in its own voice, one saturated in alcoholic misery.

Miller hovered every instant on the threshold of tumbling off both his piano stool and his bar stool—although he somehow held his place on both, upright and in control.

Hack spent a few hours every one of the next few days trying to replicate what Miller was doing. He began to come close, but he never felt he got it quite right.

After Bill Miller, Hack began copying other piano parts he liked directly off recordings. His friend Bennett was writing down sheet music for jazz flute solos he heard and wanted to learn from, but Hack didn't see the point. Why not just play them directly as he heard them? Why spend two steps when he could do it in one?

Hearing and playing a melody and chords in his right hand was relatively easy for Hack but coming up with a good left-hand part could stump him.

"Don't settle for being a one-handed piano player," Henry warned Hack, and got Hack plugging away at ragtime, stride, barrelhouse and boogie. All these twentieth century American dance styles required a powerful left hand, needed to generate the relentless beat to keep the party moving in the lewd noisy places where these styles were born, where the piano man was often the entire band.

All the old-time piano styles obliged Hack to coordinate right and left hand in multiple rhythms and intricate syncopations.

Each new style became a new exercise not only for his hands but for his mind. For each, he had to figure out its conventions, then learn to play it the right way, then curb any overthinking and let it happen as second nature.

Even so, Hack was having trouble keeping the rock steady beat which would satisfy Henry, and Henry advised Hack it might help to learn to play drums.

Hack had doubts. "I want to sound like a piano player, not a player piano. Ms. Lager warned me not to become prisoner to the beat, like a machine."

"Small chance of that," Henry said. "If I was you, I'd take the risk."

So Hack took some beginner classes in playing the drums. Learning the drums not only gave him another way to practice keeping the beat, but he got a better idea of what drummers do—that they not only generate a groove and lock in a tempo but set up the other players with fills to mark upcoming changes in songs, then throw in extra percussion bombs to keep the music fresh and alive.

Hack began to incorporate drumming notions like these into his piano playing.

As his piano technique continued to improve, Hack began playing ever faster and more intricate passages.

Henry said, "Careful not to get too notey."

"Notey? What do you mean?"

Henry said. "Music isn't piecework. We don't get paid by the note. You're telling a story. Why distract from it?"

While Henry was nudging Hack along, so was Miss Gabor. By his third year, Hack could follow the structure and hear all the key changes and thematic development of a Mozart or Haydn Sonata and talk himself through them.

Hack's exertions began to transform his experience of music. One potential girlfriend had cautioned that his efforts to understand and analyze how music is made would cut into his enjoyment.

She was wrong. It turned out that, the more he grasped with his intellect, the more the music moved him.

Hack hadn't suspected he had a spiritual side. Now it powered into action whenever he immersed himself in Beethoven or Bach or Thelonious Monk.

When Hack happened to mention to Miss Gabor his sessions with Henry, it turned out Miss Gabor knew Henry personally.

To Hack, Miss Gabor and Henry were from separate universes. It was like learning that Captain Kirk hung out with Han Solo.

Hack asked her, "How do you know Henry?"

"He used to be a professor here. He is a very unusual composer."

"I didn't know that," Hack said. "I've just heard him playing jazz."

"Jazz, shmazz." She dismissed Hack's distinction with a wave of her cigarette. "It was a very tough situation. Very tough."

"What do you mean?

She focused her glare on Hack. "Better not to discuss."

"Why not?"

"You never live under communism."

8 Henryisms

By now Hack knew Henry held a lot of opinions. Now that Henry was down to his single student Hack, like the only decent wide receiver available to a quarterback, it was always Hack on the receiving end.

Unlike his father's opinions, which Hack had been ignoring for years, Hack found Henry's startling.

Hack never heard ideas like Henry's on campus.

Henry's most disconcerting eccentricity was that he talked about God all the time. He spoke of God often and without embarrassment, as if God were right there in the room, maybe hidden inside his piano strings, ready to resonate from Hack's first fingertip's touch to a key.

About some of his own compositions, Henry might say, "God gave me that one," or, "Thank God," and when talking unbidden about his duty as a musician, he'd say, "God has his eye on me," and give Hack a gimlet look, as if maybe God had his eye on Hack, too, and Hack had better keep that in mind.

None of Hack's university teachers mentioned God except incidentally, for example, to rule God out as a factor in creation or human evolution. A few seemed zealous missionaries for atheism, bent on bending to their creed every open Christian or Jew they taught, although they left the Muslims alone.

In the middle of one session, Henry said, "Just a moment." He picked a small spiral notebook of the top of the piano. It had staves for music notation in it and a small mechanical pencil clipped to it. "What you just played gave me an idea for a theme," Henry said, and scribbled a few notes.

Naturally, Hack bought his own little notebook and began writing things in it. Some were chord sequences he liked. He even started to come up with a few tunes of his own which were not altogether terrible.

Hack created a special section in the back of the notebook. He began to write some of Henry's opinions there. He titled the section *Henryisms*.

For instance, Henry spoke often about the difference between the European and American concepts of rhythm. Sometimes he sounded like a textbook:

"Both these two distinct rhythmic sensibilities come from the human body: the American comes from the regular pulse of the heartbeat and the European comes from the rhythm of breathing."

Henry was trying to help Hack sort out the differences between playing European classical music and American music.

Henry explained his theory of the body as source for all rhythm. "The rhythm of American music like rock and blues and jazz and Latin music is what we sometimes call a 'pulse', and with good reason. Western Hemisphere music pounds out a beat that is propulsive and insistent like the pulse of the human heart."

Hack picked up his notebook and pen. Notebook on his lap, he wrote, "Heart. Pulse."

Henry went on. "The rhythm of European classical music has rhythm too, but it's not a locked-in rhythm from the pulse of the heartbeat. It comes from the rhythm of breathing. It's got a more stretchable feel, like the expansion and contraction of your chest and lungs. Especially when you play romantic music like Chopin or Rachmaninoff, you have to play with an elastic rhythm. You don't lock into a rigid pulse. If you did, it would be wrong for that music, just as its wrong to lose the beat in rhythm and blues."

Hack wrote, "Chest and lungs. Rhythm of breathing. Elastic."

Henry said, "The tell is what happens during a rest. A rest in Mozart is just that: a rest. The music stops. It's up to the players how long they want to hold the rest. But in blues or jazz or any music with that pulse, all the instruments may stop playing, you may hear total silence outside, but, in your mind, you still hear the heartbeat pulsing away right through the silence."

Hack wrote, "The rest is not silence."

Henry spoke often on different ways to play a piano: "The piano has strings, but you strike them with hammers. So piano is both a stringed instrument like a violin and a percussion instrument like a drum. The trick is to know when you're playing the violin and when you're playing the drum."

Hack wrote down, "Piano: violin v. drum."

"I know you like those simple tunes," Henry said to Hack.

"Like what?"

"Like rock and roll; rhythm and blues; folk music; country music; pop music, all that stuff."

"I grew up with it."

"Nothing wrong with it. I like to hum along with a Hank Williams tune myself. But some of that commercial stuff is just manufactured product. You know, the record companies churn it out on an assembly line, like toasters and hair driers. It's made out of the same stuff music is made out of, like chords and notes and the like, but it's not really music."

Hack wrote, "Simple good—manufactured product bad."

Once, when a bad try at some blues frustrated Hack, he said, "I guess I'm just not black."

"Sure you are," Henry said. "And Jewish too."

"I don't think so."

"You're an American, aren't you?"

"So?"

"All Americans are at least a little bit black," Henry said. "And Jewish, too. And Irish and Mexican and English and Chinese, everybody who came here, not to mention the

Indians who were already here. That's the whole point of America."

"You mean like the melting pot?"

"There's a pot, but nobody needs to melt," Henry said.

This time Hack didn't write anything down, but he thought over what Henry said, and for a long time after.

Not all Henryisms related to music.

When Hack asked who Henry was going to vote for in the upcoming mayoral election, Henry shrugged.

Maybe Henry didn't know about a new candidate. "There's a candidate named Whitney James," Hack said. "She'd be the first black woman mayor."

"You don't say," Henry said. "This Whitney James? She's a leader of black people?"

Hack answered. "The papers say that."

Henry said, "Do you know the names of some other black leaders?"

"I guess." Hack thought a moment. "There's Jesse Jackson. And Al Sharpton."

"Only those two?"

It came too easy. Hack had no trouble reciting three others he'd read about lately in the news or seen on TV.

"Fine," Henry said. "That's a lot of leaders. I'm sure we could both go on all day. Now name me a Chinese American leader."

"I don't know any of those," Hack said.

"Vietnamese American? Japanese American? Korean American? Do you know a single name of any of those?"

"No."

"Now, who you think is better off in this country? Asian Americans or African Americans?"

"Better off?"

"Come on, you know what I mean," Henry said. "Better jobs, more businesses, more money, better places to live, all the things that usually make for a better life."

Hack said, "Asian Americans, I guess."

"And you can't name a single Asian American leader, can you?"

"I guess not."

"What do you think that means?" Henry asked.

Hack hesitated.

Henry didn't. "For me, the only logical conclusion is that black people would be better off without leaders."

That seemed wrong to Hack, but as little as Hack knew about American history at the time, he let it go. Besides, despite what Henry claimed, Hack wasn't black and Henry was, which seemed to give Henry more authority.

A notion which also applied the time Henry delivered a broadside about black criminals.

After living in Chicago awhile, Hack had noticed that a lot of the newsworthy violent criminals were young black men. Chicago locals, including a few local black friends, advised him to stay out of black neighborhoods on the West and South Sides and to avoid riding too far south on the El. Although his fellow university students flagged these warnings as racist, few ignored them.

Hack learned why from a run-in on the El train. He took the El to see a game at the ballpark on the south side. Hack was standing, one hand gripping the silvery pole, the other one holding a paperback open, trying to read his book as it bounced up and down in his hand.

"Give me your wallet."

Hack looked up. Two black guys about his own age stood in front of him, a skinny guy closer, a much bigger one backing up his partner from behind. Both were costumed in bandanas and other gang regalia of the moment.

"What?"

The skinny guy said, "Your wallet. Give it."

"That's not going to happen," Hack said.

Tricky situation. Skinny Thug in front was a little taller than Hack's five foot six inches, but he was bony and didn't look that strong. The huge escort casting his mad dog look at Hack over Skinny Thug's shoulders was another story.

Other passengers preoccupied themselves with the ceiling or with empty space—no help there.

Skinny Thug slapped down on Hack's book, trying to knock it loose. Hack held on. Skinny Thug slapped it again, harder, but Hack had no trouble hanging on.

Hack thought about slapping Skinny Thug's face with the book, but the more serious threat from Mad Dog checked him.

A flare of Hack's own mad dog rage lit inside him. He let go of the pole and squared his feet, trying to keep his balance on the moving train. Would nailing Mad Dog in the Adam's Apple with his book be a good first move?

Too bad Gus wasn't there, but he was back in Ojibwa City, long finished with his brief college football career, this very instant probably relaxing with a beer at Max's Madhouse.

Slacker.

Behind the thugs, Hack saw a transit cop enter the car.

"Check it out," Hack said, and gave a head fake towards the cop, a squat wide black woman outfitted with a full arsenal of anti-thug equipment, including a big black pistol.

Skinny glanced back and muttered a ritual obscenity and headed for the exit to another car. Shooting a parting threatening stare at Hack over his shoulder, Mad Dog followed Skinny. The cop followed them both.

Hack never read a book on the El again.

At a session a few weeks later, Hack casually mentioned the incident.

Henry muttered, "Sorry that happened to you."

"It was nothing much," Hack said.

"They think they're doing something black," Henry said. "Something *authentic*." He spat out this last word. "Like it's *authentic* to be a mugger. But they didn't invent that behavior. They learned it somewhere."

Hack had taken a sociology course and thought he had some idea where, but Henry once again caught him off guard. Henry asked, "You know where they got that idea?"

"Social injustice?" Hack said.

Henry threw Hack a mild stink eye, as if Hack had played the same clam twice in a row. He said, "They got the idea from white people."

"White people?"

Henry said, "Now, who is it in American history who made a rich living without doing a single useful thing? Who prospered dealing in human misery? Who had children he didn't care for by women he used and despised? Who killed other people over so-called points of honor when he had no idea what honor even is?"

Henry was on a roll.

"Tell me," Henry rumbled, "What's the difference between making money off slavery and making money off addicts who are slaves to drugs? You know who I'm talking about."

Hack had an idea, but he didn't want to play another clam.

"Slavers!" Henry said. He stood. "Slave masters! Exploitative, abusive, raping, criminal, kidnapping, murdering, goddammed slaveowners. That's who these ignorant kids pick for role models. And they don't even know it. Those two young fools, their ancestors came from Africa and they study how to be Americans from the worst Europeans. And now we have these fools who think when they act like the old-time white masters, they're rebelling against whiteness. Talk about stupid."

Henry spun his thick body and walked out of the room through the door into his kitchen.

Hack sat alone a moment.

Should he leave? Or wait and see what happened next?

Nothing better to do, Hack started noodling on the Duke Ellington tune, *Do Nothing Till You Hear From Me.*

After a few minutes, Henry walked back in, his face arranged in a calm expression. He said, "That's pretty decent, what you're playing there. But keep your focus. Make sure to lock in the tempo. This is American music." He settled onto his wooden slat chair again. "Here are a couple of suggestions for things you can do on that tune."

Neither ever said anything again about race or crime or slavery. From then on it was all music.

9 Hate Speech

Miss Gabor's remarks about Henry moved Hack to ask Bennett if he knew that Henry had once taught at their university. Bennett didn't. Neither did any of the other students Hack asked.

Hack wasn't sure it was a good idea to ask Henry—might be a sensitive subject—so he pestered Miss Gabor until she gave in and told him, "It was all in the school paper. Look there."

Once again back to the library for Hack—the school paper's archives weren't online yet—and Hack dug into the old issues bound there.

Twelve years back, Hack found what he was looking for.

Professor Henry Wadsworth had written an opinion piece for the college paper. Among other things, Henry wrote:

BLACKNESS IS NOTHING

...Christianity is something; Islam is something: Judaism is something; "Blackness" is nothing. "Blackness" is a phantasmagoria originated by white people for their own advantage and only afterwards taken up by black people, originally in collective self-defense, nowadays in individual self-aggrandizement by hustlers who abuse this ghost of an idea to ply their scams.

As an idea, "Blackness" is a vestigial organ which once served a purpose but now functions only as a source of infections destructive to black body and soul.

The people who write and talk most about blackness pretend they're talking up African roots, but that's a lie. They use their Africanist rhetoric to hide the fact that they're channeling dead French and German intellectuals of fifty and a hundred years ago. That is true whether they're talking up

"Intersectionality" or "Critical Theory" or any of the other European jargons these frauds parrot...

...Powerful, white-run foundations and other institutions lavish grants and awards on these scammers, not because their so-called "blackness" helps black people, but because it helps powerful white people. White power brokers use professional black people—by that I mean people whose profession it is to be black—as cannon fodder in their faction wars with other powerful white people. And that's all there is to the whole "blackness" game...

...Music comes from everywhere, from every culture, from every people. There is no music strictly "black." There can't be. And, like other Americans, we African Americans have the opportunity to take for ourselves the musical heritage which comes from everyone and everywhere. We can make good use of it. We can make something new from every resource humanly available. We can make a new music rooted in and expressing our own experience as it manifests the entire human experience...

.. We cannot be expected to create the great original music of which we are capable if we are obstructed by the hostile rants of greedy hustlers who seek to shackle in the fetters of their pseudo-Marxist doctrines all artists, especially black artists, as if the whole point of making music is to be a political warrior for some fake cause and to make agitprop instead of music...

...I choose to be neither an "orthodox" black man nor an "orthodox" jazz musician. I will create any good music I can the best I can...

As near as Hack could make out, the column was one part of a larger dispute breaking out not only in the paper, but everywhere on campus. Hack couldn't tell how the fight started or everything the fight involved, except that after this particular column Henry wrote, a lot of people wanted Henry gone, including the majority of students, faculty, and administrators, which, of course, was almost everyone.

The day after the column appeared the paper's editor wrote:

> "I apologize for publishing Professor Wadsworth's white nationalist column. I now recognize that it was a truly heinous error and an inexcusable mistake in judgment. I now realize that freedom of speech does not include freedom to cause harm and offense. I am sorry for the damage the piece caused. I promise to do better in the future."

The groveling didn't work. The Board which controlled the paper voted unanimously to fire the editor.

The paper also ran a reply from Sidney Johnson, the president of the Black Students Association, which read in its entirety:

> "If Blackness is nothing, who are we?"

A prominent local jazz musician named Kwame John was more detailed. In an interview published in the paper, he said,

> "This Professor, this Mr. Henry Wadsworth is a sad fraud, a white racist in blackface. The pathetic Negro brother wears his black mask only to hide his craven self-abasement. He's spent too much time rotting his soul with that old European white people music. I know him, and he once had promise, and sure, he can play a little, but his infatuation with that dead slave master music has wrecked him. He's turned into just another classic self-hating Negro."

A Psychology Professor named Anna Psichari wrote her own column on the dispute:

> "…Violence is not always physical. Speech can be violence. Studies show that verbal aggression causes stress similar to that triggered by physical aggression and some forms of sexual abuse. Stress has a metabolic effect on the neurons, potentially leading to depression and even heart disease. Because of its effects on vulnerable people, Professor Wadsworth's hate speech is in fact violence…

> "…As a condition of their inclusion in this educational institution, whose mission is to nurture and protect, this College must not require underserved populations to expose themselves to violent language that can lead to devastating long term health consequences…

> "…Since my previous column I myself have experienced stress-inducing language and have felt threatened myself. I feel my own health is suffering…"

Seven hundred forty-three students signed a grammar-free petition calling Henry's column "hate speech" and demanding he be fired immediately. Several filed complaints with the Office of Diversity, Inclusion, and Equity. They declared that Henry's column fostered a "racially hostile environment."

The Faculty Senate conducted a fractious debate over a proposed motion to censure Henry. All agreed that Henry's column was "racist" and "white supremacist," as well as euro-privileging, patriarchal, anti-science, climate-change-denying, homophobic, cisnormative, colonialist, imperialist and transphobic. A daring few suggested Henry language might be protected by Academic Privilege but backed down when threatened with firing themselves.

Henry's only open defender in the faculty was Professor of Piano Performance Gabor, who said, "I know what violence is. Words are not violence."

Professor Psichari approached Miss Gabor and with a touch of officiousness perhaps derived from her credentials as Professor of Psychology, insisted upon her own definition of violence.

Miss Gabor answered, "I ask hypothetical question. This is violence?" and exhaled a dense billow of smoke into Professor Psichari's face.

Professor Psichari beat a wheezing retreat. Uproar ensued. The debate wandered off the subject of Henry's various heresies and devolved into a dispute as to whether blowing smoke in someone's face was violence.

Two law professors engaged in a huffing and puffing match over whether Miss Gabor's action counted as a "battery" under the law. Other academics had to step in to separate the two.

In the confusion, the Senate never reached an actual vote on whether to censure Henry.

It didn't matter. University President Drebin had the deciding word:

> Make no mistake Freedom of speech is an essential value on our campus.
>
> We are also an institution whose Mission is dedicated to diversity, inclusion and equity, and Professor Wadsworth's opinions cut directly against that Mission. We can tolerate much, but we cannot tolerate an attack on our key values.
>
> Furthermore, it is certainly the first responsibility of any member of our faculty to refrain from doing harm to students. The injurious ideas which Professor Wadsworth expressed in his column and which has

also otherwise expressed even in his classes have done irreparable harm to our students.

Since Professor Wadsworth's continued employment would do additional permanent harm to our students and faculty and other stakeholders, he is terminated, effective immediately.

So it was that Henry lost his job, although Miss Gabor did not lose hers, perhaps, Hack half-suspected, because there was no one with the nerve to tell her.

10 Making It Up As You Go

"The classical masters could all improvise," Henry explained. "Bach and Mozart were great improvisers. Beethoven too. Beethoven first made his name on the keyboard in cutting contests. He showed off ideas and technique nobody had dreamt of in 1792 Vienna."

The subject came up because Hack had griped about the time and colossal effort he devoted to memorizing the *Sonata in B Minor*, composed by the super-virtuoso Franz Liszt back in 1853. Liszt composed his piano music with the career-building strategy that he'd be the only one who could ever play it, and he was almost right.

Why memorize all those old brutally tough pieces when all Hack was trying to learn was to improvise music the way Henry did?

Hack's grousing set Henry off on one of his rambles. By the third year, their sessions often turned into Henry talkathons. Hack spent less time playing piano and Henry spent more time offering his opinions on anything which came to mind, occasionally beer in hand, although he never drank more than one.

Did Henry have anyone else to talk to?

Henry went on about Beethoven. "One time, there was this competing player who charged into Vienna. He was eager to show up our young Ludwig. A crowd of aristocrats gathered. These were the rich patrons, the ones a composer like Beethoven needed if he was going to eat. At these piano contests, gentlemen of leisure would back their favorites the way they'd bet on their purebred horses or fighting cocks.

"First comes the challenger—I think his name was Steibelt or something like that. This Steibelt walks up to the piano and makes a big production by tossing his sheet music on the floor. Then he sits down and plays a fast and stormy thing and shows off his chops and everyone cheers."

Henry went on. "Now it's our young Ludwig's turn. He picks the challenger's music up off the floor and sets it on the piano music stand, but upside down. He reads the upside-down version of the challenger's tune off the sheet and starts improvising off it. He imitates all the riffs the other guy played, but each time he tops it with some riff of his own, fancier and flashier. He turns Steibelt's whole act into a joke. Steibelt storms out of the room and clears out of Vienna and never shows his face again."

Henry looked at Hack like he was expecting him to get the point, but Hack didn't.

"Okay," Henry said. "My point, any good composer can improvise. Sometimes that's all a composition is, just an ad-lib he likes enough not to throw away. Maybe he'll take out the weak parts and dress up the good parts, but he starts out just with that improvisation."

"What's the difference, then?" Hack asked.

"The only difference is that the improviser doesn't get to fix it up later. He's stuck with whatever he's playing in the moment."

"Why?" Hack couldn't help asking.

"Why what?"

"Why settle? Why is he stuck? Why not be a composer and fix it and make it as good as possible?"

"Freedom," Henry said. "And because you want to express what's going on in the moment. Your thoughts, your feelings, what you see going on around you—what's happening now and will never happen again. There's something happening every moment you're alive, and you can't repeat it, no matter how much you might want to. It's come and gone. Your music can be right there with your experience."

Henry went on. "Maybe somebody was rude to you right before the gig. Maybe you don't trust the club manager and you're worried he'll stiff you. Maybe you happen to recall a tune you liked thirty years ago and right now it's playing in your head, the way good old tunes do. Maybe a pretty girl walks into the room and you slip her favorite song into what you're playing.

"You're living and you're playing both at the same time. Your music isn't just an artifact you make and put on display like a statue or a painting. It's happening at the time, and you're living while it's happening."

"Everything you're saying sounds like you agree with me," Hack said. "Why stop to write anything down?"

Henry said, "Get up, please."

"What?"

"Let me show you something."

Hack stood. Henry actually said, "Hold my beer," and handed the can to Hack. Henry grabbed the stool top and twirled it down one twist and sat.

Henry never played more than a few bars at their sessions, and then only to demonstrate some specific exercise or technique. It was Hack's playing Henry and Hack together kept under the proctoscope.

"*The Sunken Cathedral,*" Henry said. "Debussy."

Henry played a bass chord and a few following bell-like chords. He said, "*Dans une brume doucement sonore.*"

"What's that mean?"

Henry said, "It's French. Sometimes Debussy wrote a word story into his sheet music. It means something like, 'In a gentle mist sound'."

"On a piano?" Hack asked.

Henry looked at him. "Why not?"

Henry turned his attention to the keys and closed his eyes and recited in a soft voice, "Debussy wrote,"

"*Little by little, coming out of the mist*
A long-sunken cathedral rises out of the sea.

It emerges from the fog little by little.
We hear the cathedral organ.
The cathedral sinks back into the ocean.
We can hear the organ from under the sea.
Then only a few bells in the distance."

"Try to keep all those words in your head and tell me if they're what you hear."

Henry sat upright. He lifted his hands chest high, then lowered them to the keyboard. Instead of striking the keys, he seemed to lift his rumbling bass notes out of the keys with his left hand. He followed with his right hand playing rising bell-like chords, followed by more of the same back and forth, all in a rhythm stately and elegant.

For several minutes, the music resonated through the room and through Hack. Hack could imagine he did hear a cathedral rise out of the sea and sink back down.

Henry's piano trailed away with a final long chord in a deep reverberant bass. By the time the chord faded, he'd folded his hands in his lap. After a long moment of calm, Henry looked over at Hack. "What do you think?"

"It's great."

"Exactly," Henry said.

"The piece is great. But your own music doesn't sound like that at all."

"You sure?" Henry cocked an eyebrow.

"There's no swing in the rhythm. No blue notes."

Henry smiled.

Hack said, "And you didn't strike down on the keys the way you do. They sounded more like bells."

"They did?"

"Yeah." Hack felt his face flush, as if he were angry, though he couldn't figure why he should be, except maybe Henry had cheated by playing something so different from the music he was teaching Hack. "You didn't sound like yourself,"

Hack said. "And I don't think that's where your music comes from."

"You think you know where my music comes from?" Henry asked. "Cause I sure don't."

Curiosity overcame the irritation. Hack asked, "Why did you learn that piece?"

"First, because it's beautiful. That much is easy. And I wanted to understand it. And the best way to understand a piece of music is to play it yourself. And as you said, because it doesn't sound like me. The strangeness appealed to me. Like traveling to a foreign country."

"Debussy was French, right?"

Henry said, "I've been to France. Not just traveled but lived there. You can learn a lot from travel. You can even learn a foreign language, which is what Debussy was to me. A foreign language. A new vocabulary."

Hack said nothing.

"You can think of music as a kind of language," Henry said. "The bigger your vocabulary, the more things you can say."

"You think that piece was an improvisation Debussy wrote down?" Hack asked

"I don't know," Henry said. "I don't know how Debussy went about doing what he did."

"Do you know a lot of other old pieces?"

"Maybe," Henry said. "But it's not what I want to play. I play my own music." He added, "When they let me."

Hack said, "I've been wondering about something."

"What's that?"

"When you're improvising, like during a jazz solo, how do you know what to play next? What comes into your mind?"

Henry registered surprise. "Music, of course."

"But how do you know what to play next?" Hack repeated. "I always have trouble with that."

"We're having this conversation, right?"

"Sure."

"How do you know what to say next in this conversation?"

How indeed?

Henry added, "And then there's the experience of doing it."

"You mean playing the music?"

"You haven't felt it yourself?" Henry said. "The experience. When you're not working your ass off but just letting music come out of you and hearing it yourself for the first time as it comes out, sometimes as much a surprise to you as to anyone else. Music that never existed before and will never exist again. That experience."

Had Hack felt it? The experience of letting music just come out? Or was he just working his ass off, busting his butt all the time, every note an exertion, making no real progress towards whatever Henry was talking about?

Henry said, "There's no hurry."

11 Kwame John

Whenever Hack asked Henry when Hack could hear him play in a club again, Henry gave a noncommittal half-shrug.

Hack said, "I look in all the ads and announcements and I never see your name."

Henry said, "The music world is just like any other world. There's politics."

Hack's roommate Bennett was always checking out the music clubs in town and taking Hack to hear what Bennett picked. Chicago had a dozen or more jazz, blues, and rock venues and what seemed an endless supply of good musicians.

Bennett also did a good job spotting the classical concerts he thought Hack would like.

For himself, Bennett loved the jazz from the thirties and forties, way back when jazz was the pop music, when, he said, "They played the melody, and you didn't need to be Fayard Nicholas to dance to it."

Thin as a reed, with red hair and freckles, Bennett looked nothing like Fayard Nicholas, or Harold Nicholas either, but more like Alfalfa from *Our Gang*. In fact, he could do a perfect impression of Alfalfa singing *The Object of My Affection*, which always broke Hack up, no matter how hard Hack tried to keep a straight face.

One Tuesday afternoon Hack took a much-needed break from all his practicing. He was lying on his bed reading a Travis McGee novel, *Darker Than Amber*. Travis had trapped himself on board a cruise ship with a murderous gang of con artists.

Bennett came in and dropped his books on his bed and said, "Hey! What say we trot down to the Azure Cat?"

Bennett had an affected way of talking, which he seemed to think was the way British aristocrat wastrels talked back in his favorite era, the 1920s.

Hack laid his book on his bed. "I've heard about that place. It's supposed to be a dump."

"Precisely," Bennett said. "And they are notoriously less rigorous in carding young folk such as ourselves."

Nine that night they took the El train down to a place south of the Loop. Hack chose a side-facing seat and Bennett sat next to him. As the El carried them past the Loop into the South Side, Bennett asked, "Why so jumpy?"

"Huh?"

"You expecting an ambush?"

"I've read muggers stay away from people who look alert."

"Have you considered wearing cloves of garlic?"

About two miles south of the Loop, they exited the train. They descended from the brightly lit station down the steel steps into a dimness lit only by occasional high streetlights. They walked a couple of dark blocks through a light industrial neighborhood filled with old brick buildings which might have been small factories and warehouses.

Neither spoke. Hack stayed on the outside of the sidewalk, next to the curb, as far as possible from the buildings. He glanced down each alleyway before they passed it. Every so often Bennett shook his head and smirked.

They arrived intact. The Azure Cat came as reported, a dirty brick dump with no windows, at least in front. Its only opening was a black steel door in a passageway set back a yard from the sidewalk.

A waist-high wheeled sign was propped on the sidewalk. Someone had hung reusable black letters on the sign:

Tuesday Night Is Blue's Night!

Nine O'Clock:
Kwame John Plays The Blues!
$5 Cover

Hack and Bennett stepped through the door and held up their five-dollar bills and their borrowed ID's to show the towering black bouncer standing just inside. Without a glance at them or their IDs, he snatched their fives and waved them in.

The inside space was about thirty by thirty feet, with tables and chairs spread around and a low stage in front and a short bar on the left. A small electric keyboard and a drum kit were already set up onstage, along with a few amps and a couple of cabled microphones on stands.

A crowd of about thirty half-filled the space. Surprisingly to Hack, considering the neighborhood, the customers were entirely white—for the most part hipsters, judging by the plentiful piercings and neat beards.

Hack and Bennett took a small table at the front. A gaunt white waitress came and stood next to it. Acne and small sores pocked her pale wrinkled face. At a distance she looked older, but a close-up showed she was still in her twenties. She stared at the wall, indifferent, twitching.

Hack wondered what kept her upright outdoors in a stiff wind off the lake. Hack said, "Beer, please."

"Likewise pour moi," Bennett said.

"What brand?" the waitress asked.

Caught off guard—he'd never gotten this far before—Hack came up with the cheapest beer he could think of. "Chumpster, please."

"Likewise for me, please," Bennett said.

The waitress nodded and took off.

Bennett beamed at Hack.

A minute later the waitress came back with two Chumpster bottles on a small tray. No glasses. She handed the bottles to the boys and took their cash and left.

Bennett winked at Hack. "Excellent venue, no? In no way similar to the Green Mill or one of those places."

"It's almost ten," Hack said, "The sign said the music was supposed to begin at nine."

"Silence, my friend. Quaff your beer."

Hack did. A few minutes later, a long black man with a short goatee and a pock-marked face took the stage. He grabbed the microphone off the stand and rumbled into it, "Good evening, Chicago!"

He had a suave bass voice which sounded familiar.

"My name is Roland Summer," he said.

Of course. A Chicago jazz station DJ.

"I'm here to introduce you to the blues," he said. "Are you ready?"

A few in the crowd muttered, "Yeah."

"The real blues?" he demanded.

Louder: "Yeah!"

"I said the real blues. Not just some pale lily-white imitation, some Afro-Saxon, baco-bit, bird-turd, KKK, cracker jack Eric Clapton blues, but the real thing." He glared around the room as if daring anyone to object to the disrespect aimed at the famous but simultaneously white Eric Clapton.

No one objected.

He sneered down at a young white woman in the second row. "How about you, Betty Crocker?"

She smirked back. She was cool with his malice, in fact in on it with him.

He nodded. "Another bro-ho, I see."

Then, looking around, "No caulkie caveman Elvis blues tonight, correct?"

Silence from the crowd, maybe befuddled by the slang. Hack almost was, but he had decoded the pattern.

Roland Summer said, "I said, am I correct?"

"Yeah," someone said. A few chimed in with assenting grumbles.

"Okay," he said, seeming satisfied at having achieved dominance. He nodded. "Tonight, you get to hear the real blues—the blues played by none other than Chicago's own Kwame John."

Summer turned and walked across the stage towards a curtained doorway on his left. Another black man came through the curtain. The two men executed a greeting Hack had seen here and there, a combination fist-bump and handshake and one-armed hug, with chests held discreetly apart to limit plausibly sexual contact.

Roland Summer disappeared through the curtain. Kwame John strode onto center stage, tenor saxophone in hand. He stopped and took a stance in front of the microphone and scowled his way around the room, fixing each customer with a dagger eye.

Without saying a word, he put his sax to his lips and blew.

Or rather, honked.

As his honk filled the room, he kept rotating his head and body so that his eyes peered over his sax, red hot with hostility towards each of his paying customers.

Meanwhile, his saxophone spouted a continuous wail, passing through note after note on its way to no note in particular, not only up and down but maybe sideways too. The sax protested the abuse with a continual cracking sound, threatening to fracture and to scatter across the room hundreds of brass, cork, and rubber shards.

For something like eight minutes—Hack checked his watch twice—Kwame honked and blared and screeched at his unworthy audience.

No Robert Johnson, he.

Kwame lowered his sax to his side and gave an angry satisfied nod and strode off the stage, his shoulders and hips swaying to an inaudible rageful beat.

Behind Hack, the majority of the hipster crowd hooted and cheered and shouted approval.

Bennett did not. Hack didn't either.

Hack checked out the reactions of other nearby customers, looking for sane people.

At the table to his right, Hack noticed one in particular—a small roundish beauty with dark eyes and dark hair. They happened to make eye contact. They rolled their eyes at each other. She smiled.

Hack was smitten.

She said something to the goateed hipsterish guy she was with. Hack had seen him around campus but didn't know his name. The hipsterish guy shook his head. She spoke again. He shook his head again. She stood. He gave a shrug of frustration and stood too. They headed for the door, she leading the way.

Hack watched her out the door, his heart aching.

Bennett caught Hack watching her. "Who was that?" Bennett asked.

"That's what I want to know," Hack said.

Kwame strode back on stage. This time three more black men came with him. They took stations at drums and bass and keyboards. Kwame had replaced his tenor with a soprano sax.

Kwame muttered something to the others. They all laughed.

Kwame turned to the thinned-out crowd.

"*Stardust*," he grunted—his first word of the night—and began to play.

Sort of. He didn't seem to know the tune.

Each of his backing musicians took a different attitude. The drummer kept his eyes closed, nodding along with the reliable beat he kept with his brushes, about to drop off in narcolepsy. The bass player stared down at his electric bass. Maybe he wanted to avoid eye contact. The young keyboardist suffered no reluctance. His dark glare blazed hatred over the keyboard as he swiveled it from crowd member to crowd member. He laid one arm over his keyboard and sneered. It seemed he'd forgotten to bring his AK-47.

Until *Stardust*, Hack had given Kwame the benefit of the doubt. He'd learned to withhold judgment on the new and strange. Hack had been listening to and trying to play a lot of avantgarde music on his own. Sometimes it took a while to understand, but when he did finally understand some initially strange music, like Schoenberg or Coltrane, it turned out to be worth the effort, even if he didn't wind up wanting to play it.

After all, in its time, Beethoven's music had been new and strange too.

Henry had advised Hack, "A good test for one of those avant-garde fellows is, ask him to play a real tune. Can he do it? I mean, play it like he understands it and means it? If he can't do that, he's running a scam."

Sixty seconds into *Stardust*, Hack knew Kwame was running a scam. Kwame either didn't know or didn't care about the actual song *Stardust*, a great old song from the 1920's. His tone was atrocious, his correct notes were occasional, and his phrasing even of his sporadic correct notes made no sense.

Hack had had enough. He wanted out. He needed out. He was in pain, suffering the agony bad music always put him though. And it wasn't snobbery—anyone pretending to enjoy this clown show was the snob.

What to do? He felt an obligation to Bennett, who'd found this out-of-the-way place where they could work the long-wanted miracle and buy beer in public. Bennett was the goer and looker. Bennett was always the one doing the work of finding the places they should go; Hack just tagged along.

For Bennett's sake, might as well stick it out.

Hack couldn't see Bennett's face. Bennett's chair was in front of their table, three feet closer to the stage then Hack's. Bennett had propped his chin in his hand, his elbow resting on his knee, his unseen face pointed straight at Kwame. Bennett was obviously intent on the music.

Bennett was a woodwind player too, after all—he might be learning something from Kwame's technique, as dismal as it seemed to Hack.

But after a few more minutes, as Kwame John continued without human decency or conscience to mangle Hoagy Carmichael's haunting melody, Hack could take it no more. He learned forward to ask if it was okay for them both to take off. If necessary, he'd beg.

That's when Hack saw Bennett's face. Bennett's eyes were closed. His lips fluttered in synchronized rhythm with his gentle breathing.

Bennett had fallen asleep.

12 The Long Unwinding Road

Senior year, Hack finally ran into the dark-haired beauty with whom he'd shared an eyeroll and a smile that nasty night at the Azure Cat.

She was standing in the line for registration, right in front of him. The Internet was already a going concern, but this University wasn't going to rush into anything. Students still had to fill out paper forms.

At first, he suspected it might be the same girl, but he wasn't sure. The hair was cut in back differently from the way he remembered—and he did remember her hair, along with everything else about her.

Someone called out a greeting to her. She turned to answer and he saw her face.

He peered over her shoulder to read her registration and get her name and find out which classes she was taking.

She caught him snooping but made no effort to cover up her form. In fact, she shoved it to her right so he could see it better. A slight smile sweetened her small perfect lips and electrified him.

Her name was Lily Lapidos. One of the classes she was signing up for was called "Gamelan Music Appreciation."

The class would probably be one of those classes designed for patronizing white dilettantes to virtue-signal how respectful they were towards nonwhite cultures.

Hack would risk it. Hadn't Henry mentioned that the great Debussy himself had listened to a lot of Gamelan music? Debussy heard an Indonesian band at the 1889 Paris World's Fair. After that he came every day to listen and study, which for him were the same things. The ancient Indonesian music inspired him, or so Henry said.

Hack crossed out his entry for the "birdie" Phys Ed tree-climbing course. Hack already knew how to climb a tree. Ojibwa City was full of trees, and he and Gus had fallen out of most of them one time or another.

In its place, Hack wrote in the Gamelan class. Two weeks later he found himself standing next to Lily Lapidos with twelve other scholars hammering on gongs and slapping drums and tinkling chimes—once in a while, even in sync.

Did Lily Lapidos remember him from the Azure Cat?

Yes, it turned out. In fact, she'd seen him around from time to time and wondered why he never came over to talk with her. He didn't remember any incident like that and promised he would have come over if he'd seen her.

She hated the name "Hack." It sounded to her like a rude noise a frat boy made after too much beer. She called him by his birth name, "Nate."

That made three: first Mom, then Henry, now Lily.

It turned out that Bennett's collection included recordings of Gamelan music. This lucky break gave Hack the opening to bring Lily by their room to listen to them.

To Hack's delight, Lily did listen, with a serious attention which surprised him.

Considering himself already a musician, Hack thought he ought to be able to stun her with his Gamelan virtuosity, but it turned out Gamelan music was hard. Instead of soaring through this birdie course, Hack found himself working at Gamelan just as hard as he had to work at Mozart and stride piano.

With no musical training except for a few childhood clarinet lessons for which she'd never practiced, Lily was almost as good as he was.

Lily's intensity amazed. She stood in front of Bennett's speakers and practiced for hours at a time. Jaws clenched in an unhealthy grimace, she hammered on a pretend gong along with Bennett's recordings, trying to get the rhythm right.

She hated her own clams as much as Hack hated his and cussed like a rapper when she flubbed notes or beats. When Hack suggested that even Coltrane took a break every so often, she shook him off and kept hammering until she got it right.

Despite Hack's failure to dazzle Lily with his musicianship, she dated him anyway. He didn't know why. She was not only beautiful, but went everywhere clothed like a high fashion model, draped in silk and fabrics Hack had never heard of.

Bennet told Hack, "When I see the two of you cross the campus together, it's like a countess walking her pet bum."

She was the only child of a rich and famous lawyer. As far as Hack could tell, her father denied her nothing.

Late that final year, Lily's father Sam Lapidos dropped by campus and took them for lunch at a fancy off-campus restaurant. Hack had walked past it on errands but never imagined eating there. They had a menu posted outside— already a bad sign—which listed terrifying prices.

During their lunch Lily seemed to take her father for granted. She wasn't rude exactly, but she sort of clammed up. She seemed cold and distant to her father, which surprised and disturbed Hack a bit. She'd always been friendly and kind to all. She had a dry wit and was fun for everyone to be around.

Naturally, Hack was eager to make friends with Lily's dad. Sam was grateful. He used the name "Hack" from the beginning and laughed at Hack's weakest jokes. The two did most of the talking, while Lily seemed almost bored and maybe a bit condescending towards these two males who both adored her.

Sam didn't act like a rich guy, at least like the guys on campus Hack suspected were rich—most tried to hide it, but he could always tell.

Sam hid nothing. He dressed rich. Hack didn't know much about clothes, but he could tell that every time Sam spooned the white sauce onto his plate, he risked thousands of dollars in dark silk suit and white dress shirt. His necktie alone must have cost more than Hack's first car. The shine of his shoes almost blinded. Hack had never seen the like in Ojibwa City or on campus or even downtown Chicago.

Sam was not a musician, but he turned out be a knowledgeable music lover. Like Hack, he loved Bach and the Beatles, and also Bud Powell and Louis Armstrong just as much. He'd once heard Thelonious Monk play live at some Minneapolis club, which impressed Hack.

Hearing that Hack was studying with Henry Wadsworth impressed Sam right back. Sam had heard Henry play—he couldn't remember where or when, but long ago, when Henry seemed like the coming Big Thing.

Sam said, "Henry Wadsworth is a visionary, I think, somewhere beyond avantgarde. More like ultra-futuristic. But I hear the blues in there too. And I think I see why he's not popular. He's in that bad zone, almost too accessible for the hip and too weird for regular people."

When Hack thought that over later, Sam's analysis seemed about right. Would the same thing happen to Hack himself if he followed Henry's musical model?

In the middle of Hack's enthusiastic, long-winded attempt to explain his own theory that Debussy and Gamelan and the Blues were linked expressions of a common musical sensibility, Sam got up from his chair and walked away.

Just like that—in the middle of Hack's sentence, Sam picked his fine black linen napkin up from his lap and dropped it on the floor and wandered off, a dazed expression on his face.

Hack glanced at Lily for an explanation, but she shrugged and went on sipping her Sauvignon Blanc.

He asked, "Did I offend your dad?"

She said, "It's nothing personal, Nate. He just thought of something important, at least important to him. Things invade his mind and grab him. There's a lot of mysterious stuff going on in there. He forgets there are other people."

"Does it bother you?" he asked.

She lifted her glass to her lips and considered for a moment. She lowered it. "Yes, it does," she said. A sadness touched her face and fled. "But there's nothing I can do about it."

A few moments later Sam returned. He picked his napkin up off the floor and took back his seat at the table and spread the napkin across his lap. He gave Hack a smile, warm, earnest and real. "Go on, please, Hack. Tell me more about studying with Henry Wadsworth. What's he like personally?"

This was not the last time Sam pulled his sudden walkaway maneuver, but like Lily, Hack got sort of used to it.

It turned out Lily was Jewish. That fact somehow added to Lily's exotic allure—though Hack never saw her do anything Jewish like turn down a pork chop or take a day off for one those Jewish holidays they'd taught Hack about at Ojibwa City Junior High.

Despite Lily's outward sophistication, it turned out she was no more experienced at making love than Hack. This happy realization took the initial pressure off. It was one more area of life about which Hack knew little.

They learned together. Their early inept but enthusiastic attempts matured into experiences he treasured, and it was obvious so did she. Their earnest clumsiness carried with it a joy and sweetness which made him love her even more.

13 Graduation

Something had to give, and something did. Sometime after Lily arrived in Hack's life, his sessions with Henry ended.

The sessions just trailed off. There was some museum Lily had to show him or some trip she insisted they take together, to show off her musical genius boyfriend to her many friends, or to be alone together in a hotel or resort whose luxury Hack had never imagined.

And if Lily wanted to spend her plentiful money on the two of them, Hack wasn't too proud to object. Mutual mad love erased any doubts he might have felt about helping her spend it.

True, he'd done nothing to earn the money, but neither had she.

Bennett asked Hack, "When you think about her spending money on you, does it bother you?"

"A little."

"Then don't think about it."

Good advice, which Hack tried to take. He figured he'd get his turn to pay her back when he made some money later in their life together, which he'd already decided was going to be permanent.

Inevitably, and with mixed feelings, they graduated. Their college lotus-eater existence ended. Hack stayed in Chicago to get a music career going. Lily moved back to St. Paul.

The next three months drove Hack to despair. In agonized longing, he called her every night. They cried at each other over the phone, each begging the other to move so they could be together. But she had a great new job in St. Paul and he was trying to make it as an independent musician in Chicago, one of the musical centers of his world.

Hack spent the three longest months of his life working a day job as a piano teacher in a music school.

He hated it, but not because he had anything against his students. Well, not too much.

It wasn't them; it was him. He was an abysmal teacher, and he knew it. He was no Henry Wadsworth or Carole Lager. He had no inkling how to show anyone else the mechanics of doing what he himself tossed off as if by intuition.

Worse, he had no clue why he should care whether anyone else learned it. What was that to him?

Nights, Hack tried to break through in the Chicago music scene, where too many great pianists competed for too few paying gigs. Most of the so-called paying gigs paid peanuts anyway. It had been a long time since the Big Band era, when plentiful band jobs paid better than regular day jobs.

The only openings came at Monday night "jam sessions." Bennett advised him to play there to get himself known, to get "exposure."

Henry reminded Hack of the musicians' cliché, "You can die of exposure."

In their fanciful flights, some write up jam sessions as freewheeling musical adventures where unpaid virtuosos develop their art.

Henry warned Hack off jam sessions. To Henry, a jam session was just a way for a club owner to "sucker hard-up musicians into playing for free," or "to use an off night to draw musicians' families and friends into his club to spend on food and drinks."

Finally, getting nowhere on his own, Hack played a jam session.

It was at the Azure Cat, where they'd heard Kwame John. Hack had given four piano lessons that day. He'd tried but failed for the third consecutive week to teach the same apathetic fourteen-year-old the C Major scale, which consists of playing nothing but white keys in order, up and down.

The kid did okay on the up part, but the down part baffled him. The concept of practice between lessons had not yet invaded this prodigy's world view. Hack saw no sign it ever would.

After knocking off teaching and with nothing else to do, Hack headed down to the Cat while it was still daylight.

He hated spending time at home except to eat or sleep. It was a north side efficiency—kitchen, shower, convertible couch bed and toilet, all in a single space barely bigger than a closet, where Hack learned to sleep through the noise of scampering hordes of skittering cockroaches.

Hack made the El trip south and the walk to the club with no trouble. Inside, he sat at the bar and asked for a burger. It turned out the Cat refused to serve red meat. Hack settled for a vegan millet patty curled into a pinwheel inside a green breadish material the menu claimed was fabricated from avocado, a tasteless green substance Hack now learned he hated.

The bartender who microwaved and served this meal was the only other person there. He was a bald white guy with a long gray ponytail and an advancing pot belly. His shaggy gray beard splayed across the top of his Azure Cat tee shirt, which once might have been a pale blue.

The man's name was Shep. Shep doubled as sound man. While Hack munched his tasteless sandwich, mindful to take a slug of Chumpster with each bite, Shep left the bar for the stage and set up the drum kit and the amps and cabled the microphones.

After Shep finished his setup work he came back to his spot behind the bar. Hack ordered a second Chumpster.

Shep handed him a bottle and asked, "You sticking around for the music?"

"Maybe," Hack said. He hadn't decided.

"We've got an excellent lineup tonight," Shep said. "Kwame John is the house saxophonist. All kinds of good players are going to show. Sometimes Nerika drops by and does a tune or two."

Hack didn't know who Nerika was.

Shep leaned over the bar and said, "Jamming at sessions is how greats like Bird and Diz and Trane got their start."

"You don't say," Hack said.

"I do," Shep said. He waited.

Hack got it. Shep expected Hack to show him Hack knew who those guys were: "Bird" was Charlie Parker, "Diz" was Dizzy Gillespie, "Trane" was John Coltrane. All great jazz musicians and legendary practicers who considered a pathetic fourteen hours a wasted day.

"You don't say," Hack repeated.

The conversation hung a moment. Then: "Bird," Shep said. "You know, Charlie Parker."

"You don't say," Hack re-repeated. Shep was giving Hack the chance to prove his hipness and thereby earn the right to show he belonged to Shep's imaginary caste of hip jazz people.

Fresh out of sixteen years of schooling, Hack hated tests. Hack nodded and sipped his Chumpster. He asked, "You happen to know how the Cubs did today?"

Shep shook his head and wandered away to grab a rag and polish up the bar, dismissing Hack as a hopeless musical retard who'd wandered into the Cat by mistake.

Others drifted in. Everyone drank, but few ordered anything except the cauliflower fries.

Hack took the hint and ordered the cauliflower fries himself, then ordered a second serving. The heavily salted and deep-fat-fried batter compensated for the grim nuggets of healthfulness hidden inside.

His Chumpster was also a perfect pairing for the saturated fats.

Hack took his third Chumpster to a corner table and nursed it. Maybe the third beer would calm his surprising case of the jitters, but at the same time, he should keep a sober head if he was going to play, which he wasn't sure he would anyway, but who knew? And why the jitters?

Others drifted in. Kwame John made his entrance through the back curtain. For the occasion, he'd shelved his resentful scowl and donned an affable grin. He greeted musician and friends with that grin and with a warm hug and handshake, regardless of race, creed or pallor.

Kwame buzzed about the room, a warm-hearted host eager to make sure each guest knew he was welcome. A lot of the younger customers in particular seemed grateful for his generous personal attention, perhaps impressed. He carried himself almost as if he thought himself just another regular person.

Half an hour later, Kwame took his place at the mike, tenor sax hanging on its strap from his neck. A small starter house band assembled behind him. He announced the rules: everyone wait your turn; play only two tunes per turn; to get in line to play, drop your name in the hat on the bar.

Kwame left the stage. Shep seated himself behind the drums. First bartender, next sound man, now house drummer—Shep was a triple threat. Hack didn't recognize the other musicians, but they all sounded good on the first tune, the Jerome Kern chestnut, *All The Things You Are*, played at a brisk starting tempo which picked up speed as Shep drove it to a velocity just past the brink of playability.

Hack sat for an hour or so and watched and listened. The place filled. A lot of people took their turns playing. Some took two or three turns. A few were professional quality, especially one amazing dude who could play both trumpet and saxophone. Most were amateurs trying to improve. All made an earnest effort; no one mailed it in.

Whoever Nerika was, she didn't show. Kwame never played. He just MC'd, sax hanging in front of him on its strap.

After Chumpster number three warmed to an undrinkable room temperature, Hack turned in the mostly full bottle and ordered number four from the tweaker house waitress, who played her emaciation to advantage as she threaded her way from table to table through the packed room.

Halfway through Chumpster Number Four, Hack muttered, "What the Hell," and got up and walked over to the open pork pie hat sitting on the edge of the bar. The pork pie hat was an obvious nod to the great old-time saxophonist Lester Young, known to favor the style. Hack picked the stub pencil up from the bar and wrote his first name on a slip of paper and dropped the slip into the open hat with the other slips of paper.

A half hour later, Kwame called Hack's name through his microphone.

Hack stood and walked onto the stage and seated himself behind the keyboard. Hack preferred acoustic pianos. He didn't recognize this electric model, but the keys looked to be in the right places, and there were 88 of them. Pressing one proved they were weighted, in order to mimic the genuine article. Anyway, keys are keys. He could play them.

On the first tune, the Duke Ellington standard *Take The A Train,* Hack didn't solo; he just comped by playing the right chords at the right time. The sax player was adept, but this trumpet player flubbed his solo. He wore an apologetic look on his face, but everyone granted him benign nods and smiles: no pressure here, just do your best, we're all just musicians together, trying to improve.

They finished the tune. Shep was sitting near Hack behind his drums. Hack said to him, "How about *Straight No Chaser?*" This was a typically eccentric but brilliant Thelonious Monk blues tune. Shep stared past Hack and fiddled with his sticks and said nothing.

The bass player shook his head and called the same tune, "*Straight No Chaser.*" He counted it off and they rolled into it.

When the sax player's turn came, he played an excellent solo, but what he played seemed remote from with the original tune's odd chromatic melody and syncopated rhythm. He could have played exactly the same solo on any blues from any city or style or era.

Hack reminded himself of Henry's insistent, "Play what you hear, not what you know." Hack had heard the chromatic scales and the syncopation in Monk's quirky original melody and wove those musical notions into his own improvisation.

The tune ended and Kwame took the mike and called another musician's name and another keyboard player stepped up, a woman this time, a good pianist Hack had heard at a couple of clubs. Hack rose. The bass player thanked him. Shep ignored him. Hack stepped over to the bar and bought Chumpster Number 5 and walked back to his table.

He sat awhile, listening to the music, which more and more seemed aimless and self-indulgent, especially with the drummer Shep driving every tempo to earth escape velocity. It was a group practice session, but practice for what? A band composed of various players at various levels playing a bunch of well-worn songs didn't make for the good music Henry demanded and Hack wanted to make himself part of.

About this time Hack noticed that the host Kwame John never did play his saxophone, although he kept it hanging around his neck by its strap. Too busy and too generous to the other musicians, one gathered, or was supposed to gather.

Hack was nursing his final beer at his table and planning his late-night dash to the El and his El trip back to his efficiency when Kwame John himself showed up in front of his table.

Kwame asked, "Mind if I sit?"

"Not at all," Hack said.

Glass of scotch in hand, Kwame sat. "You play well."

"Thanks," Hack said.

"I'm always looking for players," Kwame said. He sipped from his scotch. "And you're a player. But you come out of nowhere. Where did you learn?"

"I study and practice," Hack said.

"At school?"

"Some. Mostly private lessons."

"I thought so," Kwame said. "With Henry Wadsworth, am I right?"

"You are right," Hack said.

"He's quite a musician," Kwame said.

"I agree."

"Although I have heard a few complaints."

"Who from?" Hack asked.

"Some of his other students. They come to me now and then and say a few negative things."

"What things?" Hack asked.

"I'd rather not. Don't want to dump on the brother."

"Really?" Hack asked.

"I think they mentioned you, too."

"What do you mean?"

Kwame John said, "He's been badmouthing you to some of his other students."

"I see."

Of course, Henry had no other students.

"But you know, you can come over with me and things I've got going and avoid all that."

Hack said nothing.

Getting no response, Kwame John added, "But like I said, he's quite a musician and so are you."

"Including me with Henry is taking things too far," Hack said. "But thanks. I appreciate it."

"That's fine." Kwame smiled again. He stood. "That's just fine." He took his drink off the table and left.

Hack sat a while longer, wondering about what he'd just heard. Then it sank in. He got up and left for the El station.

As he rode the El, Hack considered.

Kwame now connected Hack with Henry Wadsworth, which, if Hack read things right, meant that Hack's chances at any professional gigs in Chicago had nosedived.

Office politics. In music, just like everywhere else. The politics of winning a starting spot as catcher on a high school baseball team when the assistant principal's nephew was after the same slot.

The politics of getting to play a concert at least once in front of the university orchestra when it was obvious the music director professor and a competing pianist had some private sex thing going.

Hack felt a frustration bordering on nausea. Was that it? All music came down to was office politics? Even after all the work and study? Everything Henry had been teaching him?

He was truly slow witted. The isolation Henry himself was suffering should have delivered the news.

Hack had all he could do to play the piano. On top of that, now he was expected to suck up, too? Suck up to frauds like Kwame John? It was too much to ask.

Younger, Hack had been unable to play piano in front of other people. After years of isolated effort, he'd become unable to do anything at all to please other people. Well, there were a few exceptions, like Henry and Lily and a few friends in Ojibwa City—though maybe the only one there was Gus. Not even his mom or dad. Not anymore.

14 Minnesota

Two days after Kwame's jam session, Hack packed up his tee shirts and his jeans and his books and headed back to Minnesota.

Six months later, he was a married homeowner in St. Paul, although a homeowner without a real job.

He wasn't going to teach again. He'd started to pick up a few piano gigs, with a wedding band and more often in clubs, mostly via word of mouth. But there was no real money in that. Lily was gentle but insistent—he needed a real job.

Luckily, Lily did have a real job. With a law firm. It wasn't clear what she did all day, but she came back bellyaching without end about the lawyers.

Hack suggested that, given her strained relationship with her own lawyer father, maybe working for other lawyers wasn't her ideal choice.

She said she'd been deciding whether to become a lawyer herself. This job was in fact an excellent choice because it helped her reach her decision, which was no.

Lily's law firm job didn't matter anyway. She already had something new in mind. She was going to set up her own public relations agency.

She'd already lined up her first client. It was some kind of Internet thing, a startup called "Gogol-Checkov." Its creators had named it after two Russian writers, both renowned for their Russian sense of humor. They wrote depressing jokes only other Russians even recognized as jokes.

While Hack looked around for something to do for a living, he read some Gogol and Chekhov stories. He loved them. For no logical reason, that fact disposed him to be favorable to this startup company named after them, even if they had spelled the name "Chekhov" differently from the generally approved English spelling.

Lily was high school buddies with a guy named Calvin Bagwell who worked on the software development team at GC.

One evening the three ate Italian at a great place on West Seventh. Cal was a fervent booster for his startup. Sipping wine after their pasta and cannolis, he explained the company to Hack, "The GC idea is a search engine on the Internet. But it won't track your searches."

Hack asked, "What do you mean?"

Cal leaned across the table. "How it works now is this," Cal said. "You go searching on the Internet for something you want, let's say running shoes."

"I don't run," Hack said. "I do cross-country skiing."

"Even in the summer?"

"Wheels," Lily said.

"What?" Cal asked.

"He puts wheels on his skis," Lily said. "He turns them into a kind of long roller skates."

"What's the point of that?" Cal asked.

"Muscle-specific training," Hack said. "I use the same muscle groups in the summer on pavement as I use in the winter on snow."

"Whatever," Cal said. "Say you search for your roller skate skis on the Internet."

"I buy in person," Hack said, unable to help himself. Cal was a good guy, but he was too ardent to resist needling a little. "A guy whose judgment I trust runs a store on Grand Avenue."

Lily nudged Hack under the table with her foot.

"Do you use the Internet at all?" Cal eyed Hack like he was a mutant.

"I use it to buy otherwise hard-to-find used books," Hack said. "I got Schoenberg's *Theory of Harmony* that way. That's about it."

Cal had him. "And you searched for that book you wanted, right?"

"I did do that, yes," Hack confessed.

"And you thought the search was free."

"Seemed that way," Hack admitted.

Cal said, "But the company giving you the free search on its search engine—that's the app that performed your search—now it knows you're interested in music books. The company can make money selling that data and your identity to some company that sells music books. You think the search is free, but they're making money off it. You're the product."

"That doesn't sound so bad," Hack said. "Maybe they'll help me find more books I want."

"It isn't just books and skis," Cal said. "It's everything you search for, every site you visit. The company knows know what trips you're planning, what food you like, what political candidates you're interested in, whose opinions matter to you, pretty soon, everything about you."

"Okay," Hack said. "That does seem troubling."

"It's worse even than that," Cal added. "When you search, they decide what to show you. Say you're interested in eating Italian, like we're doing tonight. You search for Italian restaurants. They decide which Italian restaurants to include in your search results. If they don't like one of the owners, maybe out of some personal grudge, or for his political opinions, they just don't list his business."

"They all do that?"

"Not Gogol-Checkov," Cal said. "GC will do the opposite. That's the point. We're writing a search engine app that will respect people's privacy. We're calling it *Priva-Nation*. We won't track anyone. And when users find out that our competitors are tracking their searches and we're not, they'll flock to our search engine."

"How do you make this thing?" Hack asked.

"What thing?" Cal asked him.

"This Priva-Nation search engine thing."

"Come over to my place and I'll show you," Cal said.

Hack glanced at Lily, who gave him a smile of consent and said, "Go ahead. I'll take the car home."

Cal drove Hack to his apartment and handed him a cold Czech lager out of his fridge—a good start to their relationship. Cal booted up his computer and showed Hack a sample C language program on the monitor:

```
#include <stdio.h>
int main()
{
  printf("\n Hello World");
  return 0;
}
```

"What's that first line mean?" Hack asked.

"Interesting, no?" Cal said. He explained the line. Hack asked what each line after that meant and Cal explained. It turned out the program's purpose was to display the simple phrase, "Hello World."

"Interesting," Hack commented. He liked puzzles. Composing musical counterpoint could be solving a puzzle. So could this.

"Want to learn?" Calvin asked. "I can get you a job."

"What? Me?"

"Lily says you're pretty smart."

"I used to think so. But maybe I'm a total idiot who's been wasting his life so far."

"Come on, man," Calvin said. "I've heard you play, man. You're no idiot."

"That's just piano playing," Hack said. "Music for a niche market with almost no customers. Nobody wants it."

"Everyone wants someone who can code," Cal said. "And I bet you can pick it up in no time."

"What makes you so sure?"

"I can tell just by your questions. Even your stupid questions are good."

"Okay," Hack said. "For the sake of argument, how do I learn this?"

"I'll lend you a couple of books."

Calvin lent Hack three books on computer programming, Hack started to teach himself first the C language and then its enhanced version the C++ language.

In a way, it was like music theory—all logic.

Many assume that music comes from raw unfiltered emotion. It follows that the rawer the emotion, the better the music.

Hack knew different. To Hack, the more rigorous the logic of a melody and the greater the precision of its performance, the more authentic the emotion expressed.

Hack loved the cerebral in music, the polyrhythmic intricacies, the harmonic complexities, the way even a simple tune traces a logical route from note to note through chord after chord.

Emotion in music dwells at the intersection of Logic Street and Precision Avenue.

Was it Henry who said that? Or Miss Gabor? Or both?

Though, when he was playing, they both demanded the human variation from perfection which makes music expressive and worth listening to.

Back at home, Hack set to work. He hand-copied the sample programs in the books in a notebook. Then he pretended he himself was the computer. He traced in his mind each step along every sample program's logical path from problem to solution.

Two weeks later, Calvin phoned him. "We've got an opening for a programmer at GC. You should apply."

"Me?"

"Why not?"

"I don't know enough."

"Lily says you've been studying hard. Plus, I'll be around to help you out. I'll set up the interview." Before Hack could say another word, Cal hung up.

With Lily's help, Hack wrote up a pathetic resume. He held a Bachelor of Music Composition. That was it. He was bare of any relevant work experience. His only paying jobs had been crappy part-time busboy and dishwasher jobs during college and the hard manual labor he'd performed for Ojibwa County farmers growing up.

With the jobs and a little help from his parents, Hack had paid his own way. Hack had never taken out a college loan. He hated loans.

Hack interviewed with GC's HR department, which at the time consisted of a single friendly blonde woman in a plus-size pants suit. "Good resume," she said. She smiled at him. "In fact, perfect."

She noticed Hack's expression and said, "The Team doesn't want someone with experience. Experience brings bad habits. They want a reasonably intelligent young person they can teach to do things their way."

The following Monday morning, Hack took the West Seventh Street bus to downtown St. Paul. He walked until he found the right office building and took an elevator up to the seventh floor. He walked the long hallways until he found a door with a "Gogol-Checkov" nameplate on it and knocked.

No one answered. After several more unanswered knocks, he went in. There was no receptionist, but Cal was waiting for him.

Cal introduced Hack to the other six members of the GC development team, five men and one woman, from a variety of nationalities, all roughly Hack's age. The oldest was 27. The others called the 27-year-old "Gramps."

There were no offices, only cubicles. Cal led Hack to his. It was a rectangular 8-foot space sectioned off by a divider anyone could see over. Inside was a long L-shaped desk with a big monitor on it, along with stacks of manuals and incomprehensible documents.

With Cal's help and many late working hours, Hack learned.

Eighteen months later, Hack was raking in more money than both his parents had ever made in their lives. He was a hotshot working for what was threatening to expand into a mammoth enterprise.

The catastrophe didn't come until a few years later, after the marketing guy Fred Sauer took over GC and fired Hack and Calvin. Then Lily divorced Hack—not because of the firing itself, but because of Hack's pathetic reaction to it, his metamorphosis into a hopeless inert dud who couldn't be lived with.

The best result from Hack's and Lily's failed marriage was their daughter Sarai, who alone made the marriage worthwhile.

After that, Hack fled back to Ojibwa City, where his dud phase lasted until his terrifying run-in with the FBI and crew of killers broke him out of his torpor and gave him the chance to fall in love with Mattie and marry her.

All that happened.

BOOK 2:

NOW

1 Troy

"I'm calling about the email you sent me," Edwina said to the polite young man on the phone.

He asked, "Which email is that, Ma'am?"

"The one where you called my credit card unreliable."

Edwina was sitting at her kitchen table, clutching her flip phone in her right hand and clenching her left fist in her lap. Telephone customer service was so unpleasant, especially talking over the little free cellphone the phone company had given her. She had to keep moving the little black thing back and forth between her mouth and her ear, first to talk into it and then to hear whatever the other person said.

Her fingers cramped sometimes, too, if she talked too long, clutching the thing. Including right now, maybe also because she was so very irritated.

Not like the phones she'd grown up with, the mouthpiece and earpiece in one perfect-sized handset she could hold steady and convenient up to her head. Now she couldn't even get one.

The polite young man had told her his name was Troy. He spoke in a foreign accent, but it would be unfair to hold that against him. Many fine people came from foreign countries. Why, just down the street was a woman from Mauritius, way out in the middle of the Indian ocean. She was as nice as pie.

And there was that very pleasant Amir fellow who ran the convenience store before he was murdered, the only murder Edwina could ever recall here in Ojibwa City. He came from somewhere—France, she thought, or maybe Iraq. Little Nate Wilder had been the man's friend. She could ask Nate.

The polite young man Troy said, "It will help me to help you if you will tell me your name, please?"

"My name is Mrs. Ralph Malkin."

Edwina had gotten her credit card in 1968. She was the first person she knew in town with a credit card—except maybe Dr. Brown, who didn't even live in Ojibwa City itself, but out in the country, and he probably had more money than everybody else in town put together.

She said, "My card has never failed me once. Now you're saying it's phony."

Troy said, "Mrs. Malkin, I am sure we would not be saying such a thing. Probably there is being an error."

"I use that card all the time. Have you told anyone else? I need that card. Can I still use it for other things?"

"Oh no, we have not been telling anyone else," Troy said.

"Are you sure?"

"It is not our policy to do that," Troy said. "You know, listening to your voice, you remind me in a very special way of my own grandmother. May I call you Grammy?"

"I guess that would be fine, Troy. Some other people do. I mean, my grandchildren and great-grandchildren."

"Thank you, Grammy." There were some clicking sounds at his end of the call. He said, "I found the email we sent you. It concerns the Gogol-Checkov security software you ordered."

"I did?" Edwina asked. "I don't remember that."

Troy said, "I promise that you did. Otherwise, how would we have your name and email address?"

"Well, that makes sense, I suppose."

"But in any case, it is no problem. If you do not wish to continue your subscription, we can simply end it, in which case you are entitled to a refund."

"A refund? That sounds good."

"You would prefer the refund, rather than to be continuing your subscription?" Troy asked.

"Oh, yes. How much is the refund?"

"I will be looking in our records," Troy said. "Do you recall how much you paid?"

"Not really. As I said, I don't even remember buying it."

Troy said, "Let me check." A moment later, then, "I believe the amount is $100."

"Why that's very nice! I can really use $100."

"No problem," Troy said. "Of course, I must access your bank account to provide the refund."

"You have to?"

"Yes. It's standard procedure."

"Okay. But it sounds complicated."

"I will guide you through it. Nothing to worry about."

Troy did sound confident. Like he knew his job. Edwina said, "Thank you."

"No problem, Grammy," Troy said.

"So what do I do?"

He asked, "Do you have your computer available?"

"Yes."

"Please turn it on."

"This will take a few minutes," she said.

Edwina took her phone with her into her dining room. Her laptop sat waiting for her on the dining room table. She seated herself in front of it and turned it on and waited a few minutes while it warmed up.

Troy asked, "Grammy, are you still there?"

She said, "Yes. My computer is slow. It's an old used one. I couldn't really afford one of the fast new ones. Little Nate Wilder gave it to me."

"That was nice of him," Troy said.

"Yes," she said. "He's a nice young man, and I think he must know everything there is to know about computers." After a few moments more, she said, "My computer is on now. What should I do next?"

"I need to guide you through the steps to get your refund."

"Thank you," Edwina said.

"No problem, Grammy," Troy said. "Do you see the little empty box on the bottom left of your screen?"

"Yes."

"Please click on that box with your mouse and type what I tell you."

Edwina pressed the button for the phone's speaker and laid it on the table. Edwina hovered her mouse over the little empty box and clicked the way Nate had taught her. Troy told her what to type and she typed it. A new box appeared in the middle of her screen. It said,

TEAM PAL
To Help Your Team Pal Connect To Your Computer,
Please Tell Your Team Pal the Following Code:
553-5525-155

"Do you see a code, Grammy?"

"You mean the numbers?"

"Yes."

She told him, "It says 553-5525-155."

"Thank you, Grammy."

More clicking from his end of the call.

A moment later, the screen said,

Do You Invite Your Team Pal to Share Control of Your
Computer?
YES or NO?

"Please click on the 'YES' button, Grammy. You must do this several more times. Just keep clicking 'YES' every time you are asked."

"Okay." She was asked three questions. At each question, she clicked the 'YES' button.

The screen said,

Congratulations!
You Are Now Sharing Control Of Your Computer With Your Team Pal

It seemed she could handle this computer thing after all, at least with Troy's help. It was a comforting feeling.

A few more clicking sounds on her phone, then Troy said, "Thank you."

"That's odd," she said.

"What's odd, Mrs. Malkin?" he asked.

"Your voice sounds different. Almost like you're a different person."

"I promise you I am not a different person," he said. "I am still Troy."

But it seemed to Edwina his voice was pitched lower.

Troy said, "Now, please tell me the name of your bank."

"Oh. Why is that?"

"In order that I may transfer your refund directly into your bank account. That is the fastest way for me to get your refund money direct to you."

"I understand," she said. "Ojibwa City Methodist Trust."

The words flashed across the top of her screen. "You type fast," she said.

"Yes, Edwina. It is part of my job."

Odd. Now he was calling her Edwina instead of Grammy. And had she ever told him her first name? It must be in the records he was looking at.

Her bank website appeared on the screen.

Troy said, "Of course, I respect the confidentiality of your information. Now you must login to your bank account, but whatever you do, please do not tell me your password."

"Okay," she said. She tilted her laptop and took the scrap of paper out from under it. She typed the ID and password she read there onto the screen in the same place she always typed it when she logged into her bank.

Her password appeared on the screen only as "**********", so she knew Troy wouldn't be able to see it. Troy was right not to want to see it. Nate had warned her never to let anyone else know her password, not even Nate himself.

Her checking account statement appeared. At the top it read

OJIBWA CITY METHODIST TRUST

Her balance looked right, close to what she remembered.

$512.02

Below was a list of all her recent deposits and checks. The same ones as usual, the gas bill, the electric bill, her monthly social security deposit, and so on.

"Thank you, Edwina," Troy said, "Now I will be able to transfer your $100 refund into your account."

"That will be very nice."

"But I will need your help."

"What do I need to do?"

"I am going to open up a part of your screen which connects to our own Gogol-Checkov system. I will set everything up for you. But you must be the one to type in the amount of $100.00. That is all you will need to do. When you do that, we will automatically transfer the money into your account."

"Okay." She tried to suppress her anticipation, but she could already imagine what she might be able to do with the extra $100. A couple of nice meals at Berringer's, perhaps.

Maybe take Madeline Paige with her. Madeline deserved a
nice meal out, she had suffered so much lately, what with
Bob's passing. Or maybe take the pressure off the upcoming
winter's gas bill, which she'd seen on the news was going to
soar. What had she been thinking when she bought that
security program?

Troy asked, "Are you ready?"

"Yes."

Another little box opened on the screen.

YOUR REFUND
AMOUNT?

Below was a box. It contained a dollar sign with an empty
line to the right.

$$\$_____$$

"Now type in the amount," Troy said. "Then press OK."

She typed "100.00" into the empty line next to the dollar
sign and pressed the OK button with her mouse arrow.

YOUR REFUND
AMOUNT?
$100.00

Her screen went black.

"My screen disappeared," she said. "All the letters and
numbers are gone."

"Really?"

"Why is that? What happened? Did I do something
wrong?"

Troy said, "Just a moment, Edwina."

Her screen came to life again.

"Look at your balance, Edwina!" His voice cracked.
"What?"
"Edwina, you have made a harmful mistake. Very harmful, very harmful. Very much so! Look at your balance."

$1612.02

"I don't understand," she asked. "What happened?"
He said, "You must have typed in $1,100 instead of $100."
"I don't think I did that. I was very careful."
"Look for yourself."
There it was:

$1612.02

He moaned, "Oh no, no, no!"
"What does it mean?"
"It means I may lose my job," Troy said. "This is what it means. My boss does not permit such mistakes."
"You sound so upset, Troy. Please!"
"How can I explain this to my boss? Or to my wife? We have three small children."
"I'm so sorry," she said. "What can I do to make it up to you?"
He told her.

2 Sammy

"Did I tell you what happened to Mrs. Malkin?" Mattie whispered from where she lay next to him the darkness.

"Shh," Hack shushed.

"Don't shush me," she whispered.

"Your whisper will wake him."

"Your shush is louder than my whisper," she whispered.

"You're the loud whisperer," he whispered.

"Shh," she shushed.

From his crib a few feet away came the rustle of Sammy stirring in his blankets. He moaned a small moan.

Hack froze. He felt Mattie stiffen next to him. Both held their breaths.

They waited several seconds. No new Sammy sounds. Just the ordinary creaking of their old house as it settled into the Ojibwa City earth the way it had been settling for a hundred years, then a click and a whump and a buzz as the furnace kicked in.

Hack took up breathing again.

"Look what you almost did," she murmured. She poked Hack in his ribs with her elbow.

For an instant, Hack considered elbowing her back, but chose not to start a combat he couldn't win and for sure would climax in catastrophic commotion. Instead, he rolled away from her and pulled his pillow over his head and bent the soft thing double over both his ears.

The mattress quivered under him. Mattie was rolling away from him too. Several minutes passed, each facing away from the other in the dark.

Mattie always slept naked, even on the most brutal Minnesota January nights, and this was only October. She wriggled back up into him and bumped her soft ass against his.

This was no invitation. It was another of her sneaky tricks to keep him awake.

Sammy whimpered.

The mattress shuddered as Mattie tried to elbow Hack again, but his husband's seventh-sense kicked in and he was too quick. He shuffled his body to the edge of the bed. Her elbow missed him and thunked against the mattress.

Sammy moaned three times more, each moan louder than the one before. He coughed out a complaint, as if to clear his throat as he geared up to launch a major wail.

Damn. Hack sat upright and rolled over to set his feet on the floor. For the first time since pulling the cord to turn out the bedside reading light a few hours ago, he considered opening his eyes.

Sammy started to snuffle.

At about 8 AM the next morning, Hack asked Mattie, "Last night, did you mention something about Mrs. Malkin?"

She blinked at him other across the kitchen table, clutching a brown 20-ounce mug of bitter black coffee just like his.

Sammy was tucked safe in his crib in their bedroom, sleeping off an energetic night of gurgling, babbling and wailing—Hack suspected, gathering strength for the upcoming night.

"I mentioned Mrs. Malkin," Mattie said. "But then we got sidetracked with Sammy."

"I got sidetracked, you mean."

"It was your turn."

No argument there. "What happened to Mrs. Malkin?"

"I think one of those Internet scammers ripped her off."

"You think?"

"I tried to convince her, but she doesn't believe me."

Hack stifled another yawn and sipped another hot black jolt of caffeine. "What happened?"

"She got an email from Gogol-Checkov, saying she was due a refund from some computer security protection service they sold her."

"GC sells a computer security protection service?"

"I don't think the email came from GC," Mattie said. "They put her through a bunch of hoops to get her money back. But she wound up paying them instead."

"If she was owed a refund, why was she giving them money?"

"I'll let her explain it to you. You're the computer guy."

Hack made a grunting sound.

Mattie threw him a baleful look of wifely displeasure. "What do you mean by that noise?"

"Whenever anybody in this town has any computer problem, I'm always the guy they call to fix it."

"You do have a sign out in our front yard that says *Hack's Hard and SoftWare*," Mattie pointed out.

"I put that up when I had my shop," he said. "I've been meaning to take it down. I just haven't gotten around to it."

Mattie asked, "Do you realize everything Mrs. Malkin has done for this town?"

Uh-oh.

Mattie said, "If it wasn't for her, I don't think I would have learned to read. We didn't have any books at home, and I hated school. But she had all these books at her house she let me read, like *Betsy and Tacy Go Downtown,* and *Heaven to Betsy,* and *Betsy's Wedding.* I really loved that one. Every time I didn't want to go home—and that happened a lot—I used to sit on her back porch and read it over and over. I pictured my own wedding someday, to a good and decent man who actually worked for a living and loved me and his children and helped good people like Mrs. Malkin."

"Those sound like girl books," he said. "I don't think I ever read them."

"You read all the *Little House* books, didn't you?"

"Yes," Hack admitted. "I did."

"At her house?"

"Maybe, maybe not. I don't remember."

Mattie wasn't finished with him. "She was the only reason I ever got any cookies as a kid. Even when the best we could afford at home was tuna. And now you won't spend a few minutes helping her out?"

"I never said that. You know I'm going. So why are you being such a wife about it?"

She brightened. "You're my first chance to be a real wife."

True. Gus had given Hack the lowdown on Mattie's life during the time Hack was off on his adventures in college and working for GC in St. Paul. Hack was Mattie's first semi-decent husband.

"Fine. But do I get a chance at a nap first?"

Mattie reached across the table and patted his hand. "Sure. I told her you'd drop by about ten."

3 Mrs. Malkin

Hack had time to sneak a twenty-minute break. He used the time to lie on his back on the living room sofa with his eyes closed. He didn't quite sleep, but when he opened his eyes and sat up, he felt a mild rush of moderate alertness and the ceiling swam slower.

He rolled himself upright and put his feet on the floor and put on his shoes. He stood and stretched. He stepped out of his house into the morning and started his walk to Mrs. Malkin's.

It was a sunny morning. Hack took his time strolling through the shadows cast by the high canopy of ancient red oaks. Their leaves threw stripes of shadow across the cracked sidewalks. Decades of slapdash pothole repairs had scarred the street with misshapen lumps.

The leaves above him trembled red, gold and orange in the breeze, which wafted from the nearby fields the nitrogenous aroma of fall fertilizer.

Like his local farmer friends, Hack loved the stink of fertilizer. To farmers, it was the smell of money. To Hack, it was the smell of food, or at least of feed corn, only one step away from the meat he adored.

Hack felt right at home in Ojibwa City.

Hack used up his entire fifteen minutes savoring the three-block walk to Mrs. Malkin's, dawdling the way he used to dawdle on the way to school. At 10 AM on the nose, Hack walked up Mrs. Malkin's concrete front steps and through her glassed-in front porch and pressed the little white button to the right of her door.

The chime sounded from inside. A moment later, Mrs. Malkin opened her door and looked up at him through her wire-rim glasses.

Her ninety-plus years had withered her little. She was wrinkled and a bit more gaunt and even shorter than the last time Hack had seen her, but she stood as erect as he remembered. Her once jet-black hair had grayed only in streaks here and there.

"Little Nate," she said. "Nice of you to come by for a visit."

"Mattie told me about your refund adventure," Hack said. "She asked me to check things out."

"And I told Mattie I don't need any help. I've done all right managing my own affairs for seventy years, thank you."

"Mattie kind of insists," he said.

"She does that," Mrs. Malkin said. She smiled. "In fact, she's known for it. Well, you're already here, come on in."

Hack followed Mrs. Malkin into her kitchen.

"Sit," she said. She pointed at the chair in front of the artichoke-colored Formica table.

He sat.

Mrs. Malkin opened her fridge and placed on the table a tall clear glass and a sixteen-ounce carafe of milk. She set out a wide white plate stacked with her prizewinning bars, the same bars she'd been feeding Hack for decades, chocolate inside and cream cheese icing outside, each the shape of a brick, though marginally smaller and easier on the teeth.

Hack didn't drink milk as a regular thing, but out of respect and tradition, he drank it at Mrs. Malkin's. Besides, beer doesn't pair with chocolate. Even Hack knew that.

While Hack sat and forked in bars, she sat and doled out gossip.

Hack was still woozy from his weeks of sleep-deprived nights with Sammy. Now sated almost to stupefaction by three jumbo bars and the overabundant milk—at some point, she refilled the carafe—he lost track of details, but it seemed Emily Carlson was pregnant again, and one of the Olson men had died of a stroke—Hack wasn't sure which Olson, or maybe it was an Olsen—the "e" Olsens were Norwegian and the "o" Olsons were Swedish, or maybe it was the other way round?

At least they'd finally taken away Frank Lager's license after yet another DWI, which was about time.

Hack liked information—you can never tell ahead of time what's worth knowing—so he nodded through her stories for about half an hour, and a few times even asked follow-up questions for incidental details, before suggesting that Mrs. Malkin tell him about her dealings with Gogol-Checkov.

"Well, it started with this email they sent me."

Hack said, "Show me the email, please."

They both stood. He followed her into the dining room. Nothing had changed in thirty years. A small bookcase in the corner still displayed white bowls and blue plates on little stands. A tall glass case still showed off her prize collection of porcelain tea servings decorated in elaborate floral insignia.

Sepia photos of heavily garbed ancestor Malkins were still deployed on top of the tall case. They glared down at Hack as they stood guard over the family museum in case he tried to filch a teacup.

On one end of her long oak table sat a small laptop computer. Mrs. Malkin lowered herself with care into the chair in front of it. She said, "Just a moment, please." She flipped up the laptop's screen and hit a button. After it booted, she hit some keys. She said, "Here it is."

Hack bent to read over her shoulder.

PAYMENT VERIFICATION

Dear EMalkin@GCMAIL.com

Your account is Suspended on October 17. Your computer may in danger be!

Sorry that we can have temporarily suspended activity on your Gogol-Checkov Security Service. We experienced problems when it was going to process checking your credit card activity. So that we can continue the process of checking again, please help us with verification by calling the number below:

(555) 555-6237

(This email was sent by Gogol-Checkov or its affiliates.)

Mrs. Malkin glanced up at him. "What do you think?"
What did Hack think?
One summer day a long time ago, Hack and Gus had been wandering footloose down an alley. Hack saw a faint mark charcoaled onto Mrs. Malkin's back fence:

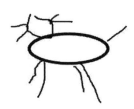

Hack pointed the mark out to Gus, who explained, "A hobo made it. Hobos mark places. Or they used to."

"What are hobos?"

"Guys who travel around looking for work."

"Like bums?"

"No. Bums don't work," Gus said. "That's why they're bums. Hobos work. They just don't have a home, so they move around the country. Or at least they used to. I don't know if there are still hobos."

"What's the mark mean?"

"It's a cat."

"I guessed that. But what's it mean?"

"Something like, 'A nice lady lives here'."

"You mean, Mrs. Malkin?"

"Or her mother, maybe. Or grandmother. It looks pretty old."

Hack pointed to another even fainter mark. "And what's this one?

"Good place for a handout," Gus said.

"How do you know all this?"

"I've been studying up on hobos and their ways."

"Why?"

"A man's got to plan ahead," Gus said, which struck Hack as an odd thing to say, since at the time they were only nine years old.

Leading Hack on the path forward as if he knew about a secret treasure, Gus took Hack through Mrs. Malkin's back gate to her back-porch door. Gus knocked. Mrs. Malkin invited them in and stuffed them with milk and homemade bars.

That first bar contained walnuts, which were icky, but it was covered with chocolate, so Hack ate the whole thing, even the walnuts. At home, he would have spat the little nuggets of evil into a paper napkin and folded it over to hide them from his mom, which never worked.

Mrs. Malkin gave no sign she noticed his distaste, but that was the last time he ran across a single nut in any of the hundreds of bars she stuffed into him over the decades afterwards.

What did Hack think?

This email lit a white-hot fuse in his belly.

Hack asked, "Mrs. Malkin, do you see where the email comes from?"

From: Gogol-Checkov <similao-indiko.nobisw56-LMLNxs.DMLNxsW@mohamkoll.com>

"Of course," she said. "It says 'Gogol-Checkov', then a bunch of other stuff."

"It's the other stuff that counts," he said. "This email didn't come from GC."

"But I spoke to someone from the company."

He pulled out a chair and sat down at the table across from her. "You called that phone number?"

"Of course," she said. "I had to straighten out the confusion. My credit card matters to me. And then, well, there was this mistake I made."

"What mistake?"

She told him about typing the wrong amount into the refund form, and how the only way to save Troy's job and his family was if she bought some Waldo gift cards and let him redeem them. Her mistake cost his company $1,000, so he asked her to buy two $500 gift cards.

She explained, "You know, these days I have all my groceries delivered. I'm a bit fearful of driving anymore.'

It wasn't just Mrs. Malkin fearful of Mrs. Malkin's driving. The official Ojibwa County Traffic App buzzed a red alert the instant anyone spotted her 1991 Ford Tempo backing down her driveway.

She continued. "But Troy was in such a hurry, and he seemed so desperate, poor fellow. I drove down to Waldo and bought the two cards. Then I drove home and called him again and told him the two card numbers and PIN numbers I scratched off. He thanked me so much for saving his job. He was so very grateful."

"I see," Hack said.

Mrs. Malkin said, "I was having breakfast yesterday at Berringer's, and I mentioned all this to Mattie, and she said I should talk to you."

Time to be blunt. "I hate to break it to you, but I think you've been had."

"That's what Mattie said."

"I'd be very surprised if you made any mistake when you typed in that refund amount."

"But I saw it."

"They have ways of faking the numbers you see on a screen."

Her thin shoulders sagged, like a marionette whose marionettist had let the strings go slack. She stared down at the age-freckled hands cupped together in her lap. In a quiet voice, "Mattie and Madeline Paige were right."

"Madeline Paige?"

"You know her. The young woman who lives five doors down from me."

"Right. I recall her now." Madeline Paige was in her sixties.

"She got the same kind of email, but she ignored it. She warned me. Said it was a trick. And now it turns out I've been a fool."

"No, you've just been honest and generous," Hack said. "Troy's the fool."

"But he has my thousand dollars."

"Not for long," Hack said.

4 Quick Change

"It's a hi-tech version of the old quick-change scam," Mattie said.

"Quick change?" Hack asked.

Hack and Mattie sat cross-legged on the dark green living room carpet, now splotched with off-white stains. In her enthusiasm, Mattie tended to nurse Sammy up to his gullet. If Hack or Mattie happened to tilt him, the sour overflow spilled out onto his clothes and the furniture and the carpet.

No one cared.

Sammy was lying on his back between them, swiveling his head back and forth to examine each of their faces in turn. He didn't say anything because he didn't know how yet. His discourse consisted mostly of coos and chuckles, although he threw in occasional random waves of his hands, like a tiny bald Italian or Jew.

Every so often Hack finger-poked Sammy in his round happy belly and Sammy giggled.

Mattie said, "A customer pays for a cheap item with a big bill. In the middle of me counting out his change to him, he hands me back one of the bills I just gave him and asks for change for that. The idea is to get all the money going and coming between us, all at the same time."

"Why?"

"To confuse me. He winds up with more than he started with, and I wind up with a short register."

Hack said, "Does it work?"

"If you're inexperienced. I fell for it once. I was sixteen. Mr. Berringer was nice about it. He showed me what happened and what to do."

"There are still people doing this?"

"Crooked never stops," Mattie said. "Just last month this out-of-towner came in and ordered a mini-coffee and took three quick sips and handed me a hundred-dollar bill."

"What'd you do?"

"Instead of putting the hundred in the register right away, which is where they get you, I laid it on top of the register and left it there while I counted out his change. When he tried to hand me back a bill, I said, 'Please wait, sir', and kept on counting out his change."

"Smart." Hack bent over and pulled up Sammy's shirt and blew a raspberry on Sammy's belly. Sammy shrieked with laughter, as if Hack hadn't played exactly the same trick three minutes earlier.

Mattie bent over and kissed Sammy's cheek.

Sammy focused his customary adoring look on her. It was reassuring to see that he could now focus his eyes.

Mattie kissed Sammy on the cheek again. "The guy didn't care for it. He got a nasty look on his face and said something disgusting. He was rough looking and pretty big. I called Spike out of the kitchen."

"Spike? She's pretty big herself. I read that at her last bout they weighed her in at 320."

Mattie delivered a stinging slap to Hack's knuckles. She said, "Spike's a very sweet person, and she's my friend. I just wanted her there as a witness in case this creep complained to management."

"Did he?"

"No, he just grabbed his change and said a few more nasty things and went off to hunt up some other waitress or clerk to sucker."

Sammy gurgled. As Hack reached out his index finger to poke his son's belly again, he kept one eye out for Mattie's hypersonic quick strike capability.

She asked, "You think you can get Mrs. Malkin her money back?"

"Mrs. Paige got the same email as Mrs. Malkin," Hack said.

"So?"

"So Mrs. Paige hasn't called them yet."

5 Assembling The Armada

Hack sat in front of his basement work bench on his tall metal stool with the short back. He'd turned up the heavy metal in his basement speakers as loud as he could. Then he put on his noise-suppressing headphones.

No sound from outside the basement could penetrate. A perfect isolation zone. Helped him think.

Normally he'd keep the speakers off and rely on his headphones. Otherwise Mattie complained from upstairs about the noise. But Mattie was off on a walk with Sammy and other new mothers and babies. She'd joined a baby walking and talking group.

Hack didn't know much about the group, but he assumed they walked and talked and cooed over one another's babies.

Mrs. Malkin had given him the two Waldo cash cards she'd paid for. The cards carried ID numbers and already scratched-off PINs.

His first idea was to use those identifiers to find out who had redeemed them.

Seemed simple, but it wasn't. It turns out there is no public record of the redeemed, either in cash cards or in the larger spiritual sense.

Of course, Waldo would have a record somewhere in its system. In Hack's wellspent youth he might have broken in to read it, but he wouldn't do that now, because breaking into computer systems was illegal—both his lawyers Sam and Laghdaf were adamant—and Hack was going to raise Sammy from outside prison.

Sammy had raised every stake in Hack's life.

So how?

Hacking was illegal, but was merely using data someone else had hacked also illegal?

It turned out yes, at least according to Sam and Laghdaf. It was just as illegal to "traffic" in illegally acquired data as it was to acquire the data in the first place.

Of course, ZNN and the other media trafficked in illegal information all the time. They claimed a First Amendment right to publish illegal leaks. Usually lies, of course, but still.

Hack figured he ought to have the same rights to traffic in stolen data as Lauren Goodwell and the other ZNN infobabes and spokesliars, but if it came to court, how would the First Amendment protect his right to nail a scammer?

Some criminals analyzed Waldo cards and reverse engineered the algorithms which generated their numbers, then coded the same algorithms to generate their own card numbers and PINS. The criminals sold these numbers and PINS.

These criminals hadn't hacked anyone. They hadn't broken into any computer system. They were just really good guessers.

And the good guessers could use their newly minted cards to buy things, or more safely, to sell their new cards at discount to other people who wanted to buy things.

So what?

Hack strolled over to his mini-fridge and took out a Chumpster and snapped off the cap with the opener he'd superglued to the side of the fridge.

He brought the bottle back to the bench, but he didn't drink it. He just sat on his stool and held the cold bottle in his left hand and stared at the slogan on its label.

Chumpster: Cheap Beer For Regular Guys

Good marketing. That wasn't what they called a "niche market," regular guys on the lookout for cheap beer.

Marketing was king. Suppose Troy's gang didn't use Mrs. Malkin's cards themselves, but marketed them? No one got rich stealing one elderly lady's Waldo cards, but Troy's gang could accumulate a lot of cards from America's oversupply of naïve and generous victims. And the gang to whom they sold the numbers could use their stash to buy expensive items and sell them, the way a fence resold the stolen goods which thieves brought him.

Imagine this chain: Troy's gang sells the card numbers to another professional gang. The second professional gang buys the goods and sells them to the third professional gang, the fences, who find ways to sell them.

Or, if the cards can be redeemed for cash, the proceeds disappear into the giant International Money Cloud, which floats high in the stratosphere above the earth and touches down on individual countries and humans only when doing so suits the convenience of our Big Tech and Big Finance Overlords.

His mind was wandering.

Short version: if Hack could find someone selling Mrs. Malkin's cards, he'd find Troy's gang. But how?

He could search in the underground Internet, the so-called Dark Web, where criminals operated online markets, and where $500 Waldo card numbers would be impulse items compared to wares like drugs and anti-tank missiles and human beings.

On the Dark Web, criminals sometimes paid in cryptocurrency. Hack had no cryptocurrency and he didn't want any. It didn't matter. He didn't plan on paying Troy's gang to get back Mrs. Malkin's money, or anyone else along the criminal food chain either.

Plus, visiting one of those Dark Web markets pretending to be a customer, even a fake customer, might draw attention from the FBI or Interpol or the NSA or the others who cruise cyberspace trolling for plump targets for their selective prosecutions.

The authorities had long memories, After his previous run-ins with them, Hack figured they'd come for him with the enthusiasm they reserved for anyone who got in their way.

Okay. Now that Hack had the Waldo cards in hand, they seemed useless.

What else?

6 Recon

Although their little family suffered no immediate financial pressure, Mattie kept her hand in, waitressing at Berringer's, mostly because Mike Berringer was desperate for help.

Hack didn't need to work. He sometimes did "investigative" work for Sam Lapidos, a computer-illiterate lawyer who rewarded with extravagance Hack's cyberspace adventuring. Hack still had a fair amount of Sam's recent payments socked away.

That weekend, between spoiling Sammy and taking to the still-clear local roads for pleasantly exhausting roller-ski workouts, Hack found plenty of leisure time to lie on the sofa, tablet propped on his lap and Chumpster bottle on the coffee table, learning about Internet scammers by watching videos made by people who hated them.

These anti-scam activists answered emails like Mrs. Malkin's, posing as potential suckers. Then they themselves suckered the scammers. They were noble knights and fighters for justice, inspirational even, but maybe there was one way Hack could outdo them.

Hack had operational flexibility they couldn't afford. By definition, any anti-scammer Hack watched on the Internet was operating in public. Hack planned to keep his action private.

After a weekend of gathering examples and inspiration, Hack was ready. Monday morning, Hack headed down to his basement to set up his own dedicated anti-scammer computer system.

In boxes stacked in his basement, Hack kept a ready supply of used computers he or Gus had salvaged, usually from the local Ojibwa College of Minnesota, which ran through expensive electronics the way Sammy ran through disposable diapers.

Hack picked his most advanced computer and upgraded it, installing a superfast new solid state hard drive and extra memory and a special hacking operating system. This took him only a few hours.

Compartmentalized inside his new dedicated anti-scam computer, he set up an imaginary computer, called in the trade a "virtual machine." A VM was a fake stand-alone computer with its own dedicated software and hardware resources. Hack's VM was completely independent of the host computer within which Hack created it. No one could tell from the outside it was only a VM.

Another plus: any time he wanted, Hack could delete the VM out of its host computer forever, and by taking a few additional steps, leave no trace the VM had ever existed, thereby covering his tracks.

Hack liked to name his fake computers after old-time major-league baseball players. His own nickname came not from his computer skills, but from the 1930's slugger Hack Wilson. Hack's high school baseball coach had claimed Hack resembled the squat powerhouse in build and style.

After some unnecessary but fun research into baseball history, Hack dubbed his VM "Vince Molyneaux." The original Vince Molyneaux pitched in the major leagues for just two seasons. In 1917 he threw only 22 innings for the wretched St. Louis Browns, who finished seventh out of eight.

In 1918, Vince tossed a meager 10⅔ innings for the World Champion Boston Red Sox, on the fringe of a pitching staff which included young Babe Ruth, who by contrast pitched 166⅓ innings. The 23-year-old Ruth was the best left-handed pitcher in the world, and just that year started to play from time to time as an outfielder, where he displayed alarming power.

Creating Vince took Hack most of Tuesday.

The hard part came Wednesday and Thursday. Inside Vince, Hack labored for painstaking hours to install detailed records of an imaginary financial life for a phantom Madeline Paige, including bank accounts and credit card statements.

By Friday afternoon, Hack saw all which he had made and decided it was good.

7 The River

Saturday gave the Wilder family their last sure chance at a picnic before winter hit.

Hack had always hated picnics. Why eat outside? Why battle the wind and all those bugs? But he agreed with Mattie they should get Sammy outdoors as much as they could. Sammy was not going to grow up to be one of those glued-to-his-phone brats, whiny and fat.

Hack was sitting on a hillock of dead dry grass, staring into the Ojibwa River. Behind him, about ten yards farther from the Ojibwa, Mattie sat on their brown wool picnic blanket, her legs stretched out in front and Sammy propped between them. Sammy leaned back against her and inspected a white oak twig his 12-year-old half-sister Sarai had handed him.

While Sammy examined the twig, Sarai examined Sammy, her dark eyes seeming to question the miracle of her new little brother. On her weekend stays with Hack and Mattie, she rarely left Sammy's side. If it were left to her, he'd never nap.

The Ojibwa was more a creek than a river, so narrow that even the shorter trees growing on both banks extended branches which traversed the water. A squirrel need never wet his feet to cross the Ojibwa.

Hack found himself in an odd mood, exultant, but also yearning for something he couldn't define. Whatever it was, it seemed to have something to do with music.

Strangely, Hack found himself seeing the sounds of the river.

Henry had said, "Play what you hear, not what you know."

Was the river what Hack heard?

The river water uttered its susurrations and murmuration, its sibilant lapping and its occasional hums, but it wasn't these sounds which absorbed Hack's attention. It was the sights.

Somehow the eddies and curls of light in the water manifested in his mind as eddies and curls of sound. Synesthesia, he'd heard it called.

Light reflecting from the water beat out an insistent polyrhythm, in timbres of yet uninvented instruments, generating tunes Hack had never heard in the world, propelling itself from chord through chord.

Was it music? Sounded only in his own mind, yet unheard by anyone? Light swirled into rhythm and tunes and chords, in no particular logical order, sounds not yet if ever made and heard in the outside world, not even written down—did these qualify as music?

What if Hack never got around to playing them or even writing them down? Mozart composed entire symphonies in his head while relaxing at the billiard table. At convenient subsequent moments he sat at his desk to take from his mind what he called "dictation"—he remembered every note he'd imagined—and wrote down the sheet music for others to play.

Between conception and dictation, while still locked in Mozart's mind, were those already real symphonies or mere phantasmagoria? Mozart was always composing. When he died, how much music was lost because not yet transcribed?

Hack had read somewhere that the music isn't thought or sheet music or even sounds musicians make, it's the information. Hack wasn't sure what to make of that idea.

Maybe a Mozart brain was just another sheet of paper— just another place to store information. And the sounds when the music played? According to the theory, it wasn't the sounds the audience enjoyed; it was the information carried by the sounds.

Maybe.

Hack himself rarely got around to writing down or playing most of the musical information in his own head. This had been true from childhood, the first time he realized he could make up his own simple tunes on the household upright.

Later, when music ruled his dreams and his life, when music mattered more than the human beings around him, Hack had streamed out through his fingers some of his thoughts. He'd even sketched them in elliptical notations, in order to guide other musicians in making actual sounds other people could hear.

Hack's music obsession had shrunk to a remnant. Now he wrote an occasional song and played rock and country covers at his Saturday night Madhouse gigs. He'd gone on to other interests, things often thrust upon him by necessity, like making a living; or by love and infatuation, like his first marriage, to Lily; or by unearned blessings, like his current life-saving marriage to Mattie.

Now much mattered more than music, starting with Mattie and Sarai and Sammy.

For music to intrude into his mind while picnicking by a creek? What would Henry say? What to do about it?

This moment, nothing. Hack got up from the hard ground and brushed the dirt and grass off his pants and walked back to spend the afternoon with his wife and daughter and son.

8 The Sack Of Troy

To go after the Troy gang, Hack didn't need to come up with anything too original. The anti-scammers whose videos he'd watched were the pioneers who'd broken the trail. Hack began his own counter-scam by following paths they'd hacked out of the cyber wilderness.

To remain anonymous, Hack started his Internet phone call through Vince the Virtual Machine and bounced the call from Vince through a series of Internet "proxy" servers from Thailand to Brazil and elsewhere. Each proxy server encrypted the incoming phone call and hid its source and passed the encrypted data along to the next proxy server. The proxy chain created an almost anonymous path from Hack to Troy's gang, who had almost no chance to trace the call back to Hack and Vince, at least without resources only big governments and Big Tech could muster.

To further anonymize, Hack ran an app on Vince to change his speaking voice. Hack spent a half hour tweaking various numbers and dials in the app to adjust his vocal timbre and pitch until the app transformed his inflexions into the angry croaks of a querulous old lady.

Hack dialed the phone number from the scam email Madeline Paige had ignored.

A young man answered. "Gogol-Checkov Customer Support. Winfield speaking. How may I help you?"

An East Indian accent.

In his app-altered Madeline Paige voice, Hack said, "I received this nasty email from you the other day?"

"I am sorry to hear that. Please provide me your name, and I will look up the email so I can help you."

"Your very insulting email claimed there's some kind of problem with my credit card?"

Winfield said, "I am sure we would not send an email which was insulting. Probably there has been a mistake."

"You bet there's been a mistake, Buster."

Winfield said, "I am sure we can clear up any mistake, if you will kindly please tell me your name."

Hearing himself speak in his old lady voice was a revelation. Hack began to immerse in the role. "My neighbor Alice says I have a big case for defamation. I could take you to court, Kiddo, and stroll out of there with millions in my pocket. And I was very good friends with Judge Olsson's father before he passed, that sweet man."

"I assure you we have not told anyone else," Troy said.

"How do I know that for sure?"

"I promise."

"You promise? Is that supposed to make me feel better, Boyo?"

"It is not our policy to do that," Winfield said. "What is your name, please?"

Mrs. Paige said, "Mrs. Satcherday Paige. My closest friends call me Satch. I have a friend who spoke with a nice young man named Troy. May I speak with him, please?"

"There's no need for that. I have found the email and I can help you, Satch."

"Listen, Chum. Please do me the courtesy of addressing me as Madeline."

"As you wish, Madeline."

Mrs. Paige said, "And I just told you, I prefer to speak with Troy."

"I am not sure Troy is available just now."

"There's no need to get snippy, Buckaroo. I just want to talk to Troy, that's all."

"Of course, I do not want to be what you say is snippy. I will check to see if Troy has become available."

A few minutes of unintelligible muttering on the India end of the line.

A new East Indian voice popped onto the call. "Troy speaking. How may I help you, Madeline?"

"Did Winfield show you the email your company sent me?"

"Yes, Madeline."

"Are you sure it's the same email I'm talking about?"

"Did you receive more than one?"

"Not that I know of."

Troy said, "Then we will deal with the email you received, if that is acceptable, Madeline."

"You I allow to call me Satch," Mrs. Paige said. "Did Winfield also tell you I am very concerned about my credit card?"

"Yes, Satch," Troy said. "We can fix that up, no problem."

"Please, let's. I have a lot of confidence in you, Troy."

"You do? Thank you."

"There's something in your voice that just gives me confidence. It's very reassuring."

Troy said, "I am very happy to hear that, Satch. You know, talking with you, you seem so sweet, you remind me somehow of my own grandmother. Do you mind if I call you Grammy?"

Aha.

Madeline said, "Not at all, Troy."

Troy explained, "Now, Grammy, this is about the Gogol-Checkov security software you ordered."

"I did?" Madeline asked. "I don't remember that."

Troy said, "I promise that you did. Otherwise, how would we have your name and email address?"

"I don't know. How would you?"

"But if you don't want the software anymore, we can just end your subscription, in which case you are entitled to a refund."

"A refund? That sounds good."

"You would prefer the refund?" Troy asked.

"Yes, please," Madeline said. "I'm on a fixed income you know, and I have gas and electric bills, and the bills are rocketing upwards thanks to those bums and crooks in Washington and St. Paul, and food is getting more expensive every day. My little Social Security benefit hardly covers half of it all."

"I am so very sorry for your troubles, Grammy. I hope the refund will help you."

"How much is the refund?"

"I have been looking in our records," Troy said. "Do you recall how much you paid?"

"Not really."

Troy said, "Let me check." A moment later, "I believe the amount could be as much as $500."

"That's wonderful! I can really use $500."

"No problem," Troy said. "Of course, I must access your bank account to provide the refund."

"You must?"

"It is standard procedure," he soothed. "Nothing to worry about."

"Okay. But it sounds complicated."

"I will guide you through it."

Mrs. Paige said, "That sounds reassuring, Troy. I knew I was right to ask for you."

"Of course, Grammy," Troy said. "I hope to repay your confidence in me."

"And you can do that? All the way from there?"

"Yes, I am able to do that all the way from here."

Mrs. Paige asked, "Where is here, by the way?"

"Where is what?"

"Where are you?"

"Kansas," Troy said.

"That's interesting. I have friends in Kansas. Where in Kansas? You never know."

"Omaha," Troy said. "Omaha, Kansas."

"That's reassuring, Troy," she said. "What do I do?"

He asked, "Do you have your computer in front of you?"

"Yes."

"Turn it on."

"This will take a few minutes," she said. "I'm not very fast with this."

"There is not a hurry," Troy said.

Hack punched some keys and sipped some coffee and stared at the basement stairs. Dinner? Nothing fancy today. Something simple and salty and fattening. Mattie never seemed to worry about calories. She said she passed them on to Sammy, who did seem to grow longer and fatter every day. And he was starting to grow hair. Did food cause hair?

Hack would cook it or buy it. If he cooked, burgers. If he bought, pizza. Then burn it all off tomorrow on his roller skis.

"Grammy, are you still with me?" Troy asked.

"Yes," Madeline said. "I'm sorry, but this is hard for me. Please be patient, Troy."

"Of course."

Hack laid his phone down on the bench. He stood and stretched his arms out and above his head and waved them this way and that. He lowered himself down onto the concrete basement floor and started doing pushups. At around fifteen, the pushups began to hurt, which is when he remembered he hated pushups and hadn't done them since his gym teacher made everyone do them back in junior high.

He stood and tried a few jumping jacks, an exercise which up until this moment he'd always considered so easy it was pointless. In context, it was rewarding.

Troy's voice came tinny from the phone lying on the bench. "Grammy? Are you still there?"

Hack walked over and picked up the phone. Mrs. Paige said, "Yes, I'm here. And my computer is just about warmed up. What should I do next?"

"I need to guide you through the steps to provide your refund."

"Oh yes, the refund. I almost forgot. Thank you."

"No problem," Troy said.

Troy put Mrs. Paige through the same process Mrs. Malkin had described to Hack. After ten minutes of fumbles, typos and misheard instructions, Troy had total control over her computer.

Of course, it wasn't Mrs. Paige's computer Troy controlled, or even Hack's. It was Vince, the virtual machine, complete with fake bank account records and the other data Hack had spent days mocking up.

Troy said, "Grammy, could you do something for me?"

"Of course, Troy," Mrs. Paige said.

"Do you see those numbers on the screen?

"Yes, I do."

"Could you get yourself pen and paper and write down all the transaction dates and dollar amounts you see on the screen? This will help us make a good record of your refund transaction."

Troy's innocent-sounding request was part of the scam. Troy was giving Mrs. Paige busywork. He'd use the time the busywork gave him to rewrite the behind-the-scenes code which controlled Mrs. Paige's screen. That way he could fake the numbers on her screen to convince her she'd entered the wrong dollar amount in her refund request. This had worked with Mrs. Malkin and who knows how many other victims.

"Of course," Mrs. Paige said. The pistol shot which started the race.

Troy had created a data pipeline into Vince, but like most pipelines, it was two-way.

While Troy was working behind the scenes to rewrite Mrs. Paige's screen in order to fool her with fake dollar amounts, Hack was also busy, racing to execute his own commands, working his way up the cyberspace pipeline back towards Troy's own computer system.

Step one: Hack contacted Troy's computer.

Head down, staring at the screen, typing with a fury, keying in one command after another, Hack was so focused he almost missed it.

Troy was shouting something.

"You are a fake! This is not real bank account! You are fake!"

The bank records Hack faked had fooled Troy for only a few minutes. Hack's two days of prepration hadn't been thorough enough.

Hack needed time to execute step two: Hack advancing from Troy's device into the rest of the scammer gang's network.

Mrs. Paige said, "Why, Troy, whatever do you mean?"

Troy was getting harder to understand as his voice rose in volume and pitch. But he emitted several ugly phrases, impressive coming from someone for whom English might have been his fifth or sixth language.

Step three: Begin moving data down the pipeline from the enemy server back to Hack's own system.

Mrs. Paige asked, "Troy, why in heaven's name are you speaking to me like that?"

Hack was ditching the trail he's seen blazed in videos by anti-scammer activists. They operated in public, on the Internet. Hack was working in private, and he had no compunctions, legal or otherwise.

Troy and his gang deserved whatever they got, and Hack was going to give it to them good and hard.

Step four: data now captured, delete what's left behind. Overwrite all their data with binary zeroes, executing Hack's special program, one he'd coded in machine language so that it would execute as fast as possible.

Did the gang back up its data? Seemed legally dangerous for them, even in corrupt Kolkata, India, which was where Hack now knew they were, quite a distance from Omaha, Kansas.

"I know you now," Troy screamed, in a voice distorted through Hack's cheap desktop laptop speakers. "You are troll. You cheat me. You think you can hack me? I am hacker, not you!"

Hack leaned back in his stool and took a swig of his Chumpster, which had turned tepid. He hated warm beer. Would have go get a cold one.

"You will not cheat me, mother! You will not cheat me!"

It is striking the righteous indignation criminals summon when someone "cheats" them out of their loot.

"You're too late, Troy," Mrs. Paige said. Hack wasn't going to repeat the blunder Odysseus made three thousand years ago, when, after blinding the one-eyed Cyclops, he revealed his true name to the monster.

Instead, Mrs. Paige cooed, "I already have your data. And your money, too, by the way, Now you can honestly tell people you've lost your job, such as it was, because you've got no company."

All true. Hack had it all, including the names of all the gang's past victims and the dollar amounts the gang had scammed, the email addresses, the phone numbers, and all the identity information any identity thief could desire, as well as a lot more.

And the gang had none of it anymore.

"What you talking? You I will f—"

Mrs. Paige hung up.

Hack closed Vince and spent the next thirty minutes erasing Vince from his computer and erasing all evidence Vince had ever existed.

Troy and his gang were broke.

And Hack? Hack had siphoned their cash into a Cayman Islands account of his own. The cash amount wasn't that great, twenty-five thousand dollars and change.

But Hack had their cryptocurrency too. He hadn't expected that. But they kept the private decryption key to their crypto in a secured file on their network. One of the few things he knew about cryptocurrency was that his sole possession of the private key now gave him total control over the crypto. It was all Hack's money now, to spend as he wished.

Hack poured the dead beer into the laundry sink and got himself a fresh cold one and sipped it in satisfaction as he browsed through his new treasures.

9 I.O.R.R.R.R.: Professor Hugh Duffy

Like good Germans, Troy's gang kept comprehensive records of their crimes. Their data included the amount scammed from each victim as well as complete bank account information, such as income sources and monthly expenses. The kicker was the victim's identity information, including social security number, which would have come in handy for future identity theft, mostly likely in the planning stages already.

The data in their records totaled up to more than $206,000 U.S., stolen from 202 victims.

How get the money back to the victims? Hack could find a way to return the cash to Mrs. Malkin and a few of the other victims, but the twenty-five thousand dollars cash was nowhere near enough.

The cryptocurrency for which Hack held the private key? Hack had no idea what that was worth, or even how to retrieve it.

Simple subtraction--$206,000 minus $25,000—suggested the cryptocurrency might be worth about $180,000.

Among the 202 victims, he recognized three names of people he knew: Edwina Malkin, Aviva Lapidos and Henry Wadsworth—if this was the same Henry Wadsworth Hack had known.

Start with the cash and take it as far as it would go.

Returning Mrs. Malkin's thousand dollars was easy. That afternoon he walked the three blocks to her house and stuck an envelope with the cash through her front door mail slot. Hack would reimburse himself from the Troy Gang money he'd moved to the Caymans.

Henry Wadsworth had lost $300.00. Was this Hack's Henry? Hack had no idea where his Henry was, or if he was even alive. This was a special case. For now, Hack put off dealing with it.

For the victims he didn't know personally, why not just call them?

He created a spreadsheet which included every victim's name, contact information, and amount stolen. He sorted the 202 victims on the spreadsheet in order of dollar amount stolen, the largest first.

Since he had enough from the Cayman money to cover the two other local Ojibwa City victims, he started with them.

The first was Hugh Duffy. A little Internet research revealed that Hugh Duffy was The Andrew Clyde Endowed Professor of Economics at Ojibwa City College of Minnesota.

It took Hack only an hour to create a new virtual machine he dubbed Vince II. Once again, he routed his Internet call from Vince through a series of proxy servers to Professor Duffy's home number. This time he used his voice-altering app to create the cadence and pitch of a young woman, chipper and efficient.

The phone rang several times before it was answered. "Hello?" A hesitant male voice.

"Hello. I am Ms. Clarissa Kent. I'm calling on behalf of I.O.R.R.R.R., the International Organization for Reimbursement, Redistribution, Reparation and Reconciliation. We're an international 501(c)3 tax-deductible non-profit Non-Governmental Organization. Do I have the pleasure of speaking with Professor Hugh Duffy?"

"Yes, but I can't really talk now."

"This is about money, Professor Duffy."

"Is this about that grant screw-up again? It was an honest mistake. I've already promised the Board I'll straighten that out. I just need a little more time. I'm collecting the receipts even as we speak. Please just give me a little more time."

"No, it's not about that," Ms. Kent said, "I am calling to offer you a significant sum of money."

"Really? How much?"

Ms. Kent said. "I believe you lost eleven thousand dollars this past June in a spurious telephone conversation and subsequent Internet encounter."

"You mean that phone call from Gogol-Checkov?"

"Yes, that phone call," Ms. Kent said. "But I'm sure by now you've figured out that it was not Gogol-Checkov."

"I have," Professor Duffy said. "How did you find out about it?"

"Please don't concern yourself, Professor Duffy. The point is that we are in a position to reimburse you the entire amount lost."

"Really? Let me think for a moment."

Ms. Kent asked, "Is there an issue?"

"I'm on the College Investment Advisory Council and the Board of Directors. We manage investments for the College Endowment. I also advise many other Funds, such as the Mike Kelly World Beating Hedge Fund. I have important clients, clients whose names would impress you."

Hack doubted that, but Ms. Kent said, "That is impressive."

Duffy went on. "I would prefer that no one find out about the phone call and its unfortunate aftermath. Such an inconvenient incident might tarnish my professional reputation. You haven't told anyone, have you? I am a highly esteemed investment advisor."

"All our activities are completely confidential," Ms. Kent reassured the highly esteemed investment adviser.

"Just who did you say you are again?"

"Clarissa Kent of the I.O.R.R.R.. We're an international 501(c)3 tax-deductible non-profit Non-Governmental Organization. One of our Justice missions is to reimburse money to the wrongfully-exploited and marginalized."

"And that's me?"

'It appears so."

"How was that decided?"

"I'm not in a position to know," Ms. Kent said. "Those determinations come from a different department. I just provide the good news to our fortunate recipients and manage disbursement of the reimbursements. How would you like that done?"

"Will there be a record?"

"A record of the transaction?"

"Yes," Duffy said.

"Not at our end, As I say, we operate with total confidentiality. But I cannot rule that out. Perhaps in your own bank, for example."

"I see," Duffy said. A pause, then, "Thanks, but I decline."

"I don't understand."

"Let's just say that from my point of view, this entire unfortunate situation is better lost and forgotten. Never happened."

"Professor, I am offering you money. Eleven thousand dollars. In any form you want, direct deposit, cash, whatever works best for you."

"Thanks, but no thanks." Professor Duffy hung up.

Well, that was special. On his spreadsheet, Hack put a checkmark by the name of the highly esteemed investment advisor.

10 *I.O.R.R.R.R.: Director S. Jackson-Wendt*

How about the other local Ojibwa City name—S. Jackson-Wendt?

Probably a woman. Most who hid their first names were women. Made sense, actually.

On his spreadsheet, Hack saw Jackson-Wendt's name listed with seven scams spread over seven months:

June 7	-	$300
July 12	-	$500
July 29	-	$900
August 5	-	$1,900
August 22	-	$1,400
September 3 -		$1,500
October 4	-	$2,300

Who'd fall for the same trick seven times?

An Ojibwa College administrator, it turned out. Hack found S. Jackson-Wendt's name on the Ojibwa College of Minnesota website. It turned out the College had 1,047 enrolled students who studied under 91 instructors, including 45 professors, 31 Assistant Professors and 15 others.

Along with its 91 teachers, the College also employed 94 administrators, almost half of whom worked for the Department of Diversity, Inclusion and Equity. One of the diversicrats was S. Jackson-Wendt, identified as Director of Inclusion, an office included in the Office of Diversity. Inclusion and Outreach, which was one part of the Department of Diversity Inclusion and Institutional Equity.

The list of institutional department and position titles were very confusing, Hack suspected intentionally.

The "Office of Diversity, Inclusion and Outreach" was a different office from the "Office of Diversity and Inclusion," whose various provosts, presidents, vice presidents and directors seemed to consider Outreach beneath them.

S. Jackson-Wendt's department actually had five Directors, as well as three Executive Directors and four Provosts, if you counted the Vice Provost, the Assistant Provost, and the Associate Provost.

Did Associate rank higher than Assistant? Who knew? Operating on his own for years, Hack had always been his own Assistant and Associate as well as his own Director and Provost and President. Saved him the trouble of worrying about diversity, inclusion and equity.

A little research showed that every diversicrat received a salary bigger than any Hack ever earned when he designed and developed the search engine which had turned his then-employer Gogol-Checkov into a cash-generating Big Tech giant.

This fact irked.

Tuition at the College had doubled in the past five years. Now Hack knew why.

By contrast, the College Engineering Department employed only three professors and one instructor. Chemistry had one teacher, a lowly Assistant Professor. Not even an Associate, assuming that was higher.

All Hack's reconnaissance figured into deciding how to approach S. Jackson-Wendt. Hack popped the cap off his second Chumpster of the afternoon and did some hard thinking. A third of his way through this second bottle, he made his decision. He adjusted his voice-altering app's dials until he arrived at the prissy cadence and adenoidal timbre of a Gen Z SJW soyboy. Then he made the call.

No answer for six rings. Then, in a robot-like female voice, "I'm unavailable right now. Please leave a message at the beep."

At the beep, Hack said, "Hello. I am Channing Adams from I.O.R.R.R.R., the International Organization for Reimbursement, Redistribution, Reparation and Reconciliation. We are an international 501(c)3 tax-deductible non-profit Non-Governmental Organization. One prong in our multi-pronged Justice mission is to reimburse those victimized across international borders. I'd like to—"

"Hello?" A woman's voice cut in. "Hello?"

"Oh," Channing said. "I apologize. I thought you were unavailable."

"I just use the machine to screen my calls," she said. "There are a lot of white supremacists out there. I must take care."

"I'm sorry to hear that." Channing Adams apologized sorrowfully.

"It is to be expected," she bemoaned her situation. "I've ruffled a lot of white nationalist feathers. And they run Ojibwa City, like so much of America. I make it a practice to preview my messages so I can hear who's calling. Then I decide whether to answer. Who is this again?"

"I am Channing Adams of I.O.R.R.R,R., the International Organization for Reimbursement, Redistribution, Reparation and Reconciliation. We are an international 501(c)3 tax-deductible non-profit Non-Governmental Organization. One prong of our multi-pronged Justice mission is to reimburse those victimized across international borders."

"Like who?"

"I am sorry." Channing apologized again. "But our records indicate that in June, twice again in July, twice again in August, then in September and even in October, you have been scammed by an international Internet scamming ring."

"Records? Where did you get these records?"

"I admit I don't know," Channing admitted.

"You don't know? How can that be?"

"I am sorry," Channing said sorrowfully. "But that is not any aspect of my duties. Somebody else does that. I work in the reimbursement and reparation and reconciliation and redistribution department."

"And how is this matter any concern of the I.O.R.R.R.R.?"

"I'm sorry?" Channing apologized sorrowfully again.

"What business is it of your organization where someone's money goes?"

"One of our missions is to reimburse victims of international crime."

"And you're going to save the rest of us, is that correct?

"I confess that I am confused." he confessed confusedly.

"Don't you understand?"

"Understand what?" Because Channing didn't. Even Hack didn't.

"What it means to decolonize?"

"I think I read something about it in my Decolonization Studies class."

"Then you should recognize it when you see it. My work is part of an ongoing effort to decolonize the wealth the West stole from colonized countries like India."

"Yes, I acknowledge that was terrible," Channing acknowledged. "We have much to make amends for."

"To decolonize and not merely diversify," she reminded Channing Adams, "We must recognize that, like knowledge, money is inevitably marked by power relations. A decolonized banking system will bring questions of class, caste, race, gender roles, ability and sexuality into dialog with each other, instead of pretending that there is some kind of generic entity called money which exists apart from those more fundamental realities."

Sounded like she was reading aloud from something.

Which she confirmed. "I wrote that. It's from my Thesis on Economics."

I bet it is, Hack thought. On the other hand, Channing was plaintive. "Lamentably, you're being scammed," he lamented. "You're losing your money to fraudsters. How can you afford that, month after month?"

"Oh, it's not my money."

"It isn't?"

"No. Of course not. I am the DODO."

For an instant, Hack wondered who was trolling whom.

Channing asked her, "The Dodo?"

"Director Of Decolonization Outreach," she said.

Channing asked, "You do this a lot?"

"We've set up a fund to disburse money to India and other former colonies of western imperialist countries. It's a form of equitable redistribution."

"Where does the money come from? The government?"

"Primarily," she said. "And supplemented by a private fund. Contributions from prosperous white people newly woken to the crimes of their ancestors."

"I must apologize again," Channing conceded, the most apologetically yet. "But I hope you understand I was just trying to help."

"Listen, I am a strong independent woman."

"That's wonderful to hear," Channing said admiringly. "And I admire it."

"I don't need your approval," she said disapprovingly. "And I don't need your patriarchal condescension, or the help of any of the rest of you white supremacist hetero male saviors."

Time for Channing to show some gumption? "That's offensive."

"What do you mean?"

"You're assuming my gender, aren't you?"

"What?"

"You think because of my name and my voice and my beard—"

"I can't even see your beard!"

"Well, I have one!" Channing cried. "Not that it reduces in anyway my fundamental femaleness. How dare you!"

And hung up.

Okay.

Two victims in, Hack could see that returning the money might turn into a painful process.

Hack's cell phone rang. The screen showed it was Mrs. Malkin. He clicked it on. Before he said a word, she said, "I know it was you, Nate."

"Who was me?"

"It was you who dropped that cash through my front door mail slot, wasn't it?"

"Yes, it was."

A day for confessions, it seemed. Or maybe Hack hadn't yet shaken off his Channing Adams persona.

"I've been fretting all day," Mrs. Malkin said. "You didn't take that money out of your own pocket, did you?"

"No, that came from the scammers."

"Really?"

"Honest, Mrs. Malkin. It's your money, not mine."

"I would love to know how you did that," she said, "but I probably wouldn't understand. I'll just say thank you and ask you to drop by this afternoon. Bring Mattie too, and I'd love to see little Sammy again. He's cute as a button. I've just baked up a new batch of bars, the kind you love."

Finally, a conversation that made sense.

11 Sam Lapidos

Hack's spreadsheet included Sam's new wife Aviva Lapidos, taken for $400.

Saturday afternoon, Hack made the call and heard only a message: "Hi. This is Sam Lapidos. It's Shabbat, and I can't speak with you just now. I'll check my messages after sundown Saturday. If this is an emergency, please call my partner Jacob Laghdaf at 651-555-1234. He's not Jewish."

Sam observing the Jewish Sabbath? Maybe Aviva's influence.

Hack said, "Hi Sam. Please call me when you have a moment. It actually matters," and hung up.

Around 8 PM that night, Hack was on stage at Max's Madhouse, setting up his keyboard for his band's regular Saturday night gig. His cell rang. Hack answered. "I'm at work, Sam."

"You called. You said it matters."

"I was browsing through a database of victims kept by a gang of Internet scammers, and—"

Sam interrupted. "How'd you get hold of something like that?"

Sam the lawyer—always asking questions people didn't want to answer, at least people like Hack. "Doesn't matter. The point is I ran across the name Aviva Lapidos."

"My bride?"

"I'm afraid so."

"How much did she get taken for?"

"Four hundred." Hack explained the Troy Gang scam and how it worked.

Sam sighed. "I see. She's not very sophisticated about computer things."

"Neither are you," Hack reminded him.

134

Sam said, "I'll talk to her."

"I ran across another name too. Henry Wadsworth."

Hack recalled an enthusiastic conversation in the distant past about Henry Wadsworth music. One of the few times Hack impressed Sam was mentioning that Wadsworth was Hack's teacher.

"Henry Wadsworth is a more common name than Aviva Lapidos," Sam said. "Are you sure it's your Henry Wadsworth?"

"No idea," Hack said. "But I'll find out."

"Let me know when you do," Sam said. "How are Mattie and Sammy?"

"Great."

"I was kind of flattered, you know, hearing that you named him Sammy. Did you name him after me? There's no reason you should know this, but we Jews don't generally name someone after a living person."

"Why not?"

"The reasons are murky, at least to me. Let's say it invites trouble."

"No worry," Hack said. "The name on his birth certificate is Amir."

"After Amir Muhammed? Your Muslim friend who was murdered a couple of years ago?"

"Yes," Hack said. "But we can't have people calling him Ammy. Might make trouble in school. We decided his nickname is Sammy."

"Makes some sense," Sam said. He paused. "And how are Lily and Sarai?"

"Don't you know? I mean, Lily's only my ex-wife. She's your daughter. Anyway, I see Sarai all the time, on weekends and as many other times as I can—she's with me at the Madhouse right now, in fact--but I see Lily mostly when we pass Sarai back and forth. We don't talk that much."

"I know all that, of course."

"Yes you do."

Another pause. Weird. A typical conversation with Sam Lapidos ended in the middle, when Sam decided it was over and hung up or, if in person, sprinted out of the room. Why was Sam dragging this one out? And he sounded even more jittery than usual.

"You sound antsy," Hack said. "Are you in trial?"

"No," Sam said. "Not yet. But I've got one coming up. I admit it's troubling me."

"How come?"

"Well, you know, the Feds usually convict."

"Why is that?"

Sam said, "They have all the advantages."

"Like guilt?

"I was thinking more along the lines of all their resources," Sam said. "Like staff and money and willingness to lie."

"I know," Hack agreed, having experienced the FBI's willingness to lie. "But you'll do fine."

This was Hack's oddest conversation with Sam ever. It kept dragging on. Hack asked, "Is there something else you want to tell me?"

"Yes. There is something else."

"Okay."

"And I'm not sure how to tell Lily and Sarai."

"Warm up by telling me."

"It seems Aviva is pregnant."

"It seems?"

"All right, it's medically confirmed," Sam said.

"Aren't you a little old for that?"

"It seems I am not. But more to the point, it seems Aviva is also not. And it seems she is the one who matters, biologically, it seems."

"Well, Mazal Tov. Aren't you thrilled?"

"Of course I am. I'm just not sure how to tell Lily and Sarai, or how they'll react."

"They'll react great," Hack said. "Sarai never stopped pestering us for a little brother. When she gets hold of Sammy, we can't pry him loose. She'll love having another sister or brother."

"Aunt or uncle, you mean. I am her grandfather, after all."

"Good point," Hack said. "But a baby's a baby, right? She'll love it. And so will Lily. Maybe this'll give her something new to talk about in place of that novel she's always yammering on about but never finishes."

"You sure Sarai and Lily will be happy about this?"

Hack considered.

Sarai? For sure.

Lily? Maybe.

Hack said, "Sure I'm sure. It's great news all around."

"It's the weekend. You said Sarai is there with you right now?"

Hack glanced around. Gus was just coming through the back door, carrying his bass and bass amp. Mel was kneeling behind Hack on their small stage, setting up his drum kit. Baz never arrived until five minutes before they played.

Hack spotted Sarai bending over the pool table, running her own scam against a few locals, who never suspected until it was too late that a twelve-year-old girl could run the table right out of the break the way she could. She had her own private pool table at Lily's spacious home in St. Paul, along with a foosball table, a ping pong table, and three old-time pinball machines. Hack was jealous.

At least the pool table had a practical side.

"Sure, Sarai's here," Hack said. "Mattie's home with Sammy. They'll switch places when it gets time for Mattie to come in and sing."

"So, you could be the one to tell Sarai?" Sam asked.

"No, I couldn't be the one to tell Sarai," Hack said. "That's your job. And Lily too, in case you were about to ask."

Sam—with a judge and jury, never fazed. With his own daughter and granddaughter—permanent fazement. Probably with Aviva too.

Sam sighed. "I'll call and tell them both soon."

"How soon?"

"Pretty soon."

"Anyway, it's great news," Hack said. "Congratulations. And give Aviva my love and congratulations too. Which reminds me."

"Of?"

"How do you want me to get the scammed four hundred dollars back to you?"

Sam's lawyer brain kicked in again. "Am I to infer that by some as-yet-unexplained means fair or foul, you not only got the scammers' business records but their money as well?"

"Only some of their money, as far as I can tell."

"I don't follow."

"Only some of the money's in cash. The rest is cryptocurrency. I don't know what it's worth. You know anything about crypto?"

"Not a thing, but I bet Laghdaf does."

"You're right," Hack said. "I should have thought of that."

"Yes, you should have," Sam said. "As of right now you don't have the cash to cover everyone's losses?"

"Not yet," Hack said.

"For now, refund the four hundred cash to someone who needs it right away. Put us at the back of the line."

"You don't want your money back?"

"Are you crazy? Of course I want our money back," Sam said. "I'm not going to let anyone rob us. But it's not an immediate need. We'll wait until you get it all back."

"What if I don't get it all back?"

"I know you. You will." Sam clicked off.

Sarai breezed over to Hack, counting the wad of cash in her small hands, her dark eyes bright with pre-teen greed. She asked, "Who were you talking to, Dad?"

"Your grandfather."

"Really? Any news?"

"Nothing I need to pass on," Hack said. "You should call him yourself tomorrow. He'll love that."

12 Max's Madhouse

Just before the gig, Hack drove Sarai home to care for Sammy and brought Mattie back to the Madhouse to sing.

Mattie sang great. On his drums, Mel grooved in that sweet spot right on the back edge of the beat. Gus plucked tasteful bass notes and Baz rattled the walls with earsplitting guitar riffs.

Hack coasted through the gig. He was playing the same rock and country tunes he'd played hundreds of times before. His hands and fingers did the work as his attention wandered from face to face in the crowd. For the thousandth time, he wondered as he wandered what listeners were experiencing inside their heads while he and his friends made their organized noise.

Came midnight, after their third set. Most customers had drifted home, but Max insisted they play until 1:30 AM. The band would have to play one short final set after this final break.

Hack and friends took their usual seats at their usual table for six in the back of the club. Mattie sat to Hack's left at one end of the table, Gus and Sylvia were across from Hack, Rolf Johnson sat to Hack's right and Rolf's wife Debra took the other end of the table, to Rolf's right.

They were drifting through another of the meandering conversations the bunch indulged in every Saturday night.

Everybody nursed a Chumpster but Mattie, who sucked on one of Max's special smoothies through a double-wide straw—she didn't want Sammy to develop a beer habit through her milk.

As usual, Gus had been doing most of the talking. He sat huge and hairy, his big protruding knuckles bulging around his beer bottle. Sylvia was a blonde woman, large herself but not

140

at all hairy, except for the voluminous blonde hair on the top of her head where it belonged. Rolf was not as tall as Gus but thicker and wider.

Rolf steadfastly maintained a cop's noncommittal expression on his obsidian face. Debra was a Deputy too, but one notion after another animated hers.

Mattie was Mattie, so familiar Hack no longer remembered how she looked to other people, except, he assumed, beautiful.

Rolf said, "You know, I think you guys are playing better than usual tonight."

"Really?" Gus asked. "I think we play pretty well every week."

"Sometimes it's better than other times," Rolf said.

"It's always pretty good," Gus said.

"Not going to argue," Rolf said. He tipped his bottle in small salute. "Whatever you say, sir."

From next to Gus, Sylvia asked, "Rolf, why do you do that?"

"Do what?" Rolf asked.

"Call everyone 'sir' all the time?" She shrugged a smile as if to signal, no offense intended. "No one on Planet Earth calls Gus 'sir'."

"You sure don't," Gus said to her.

Rolf shrugged. "Habit, I guess. From my job."

Sylvia asked, "Because you're a cop?"

"Deputy Sheriff," Rolf said.

"Same difference," Sylvia said. "But do all you law enforcement people do that? Call everyone 'sir'?"

"We call people sir and ma'am because we hope that if we address them with respect they'll behave like people who deserve respect," Rolf said.

"You mean obey you," Sylvia said.

Rolf nodded. "Another way of putting it."

"But even here at the Madhouse, in a personal conversation?" Sylvia asked. "Who's going to obey you when you're off duty?"

"Like I said, habit," Rolf said.

Sylvia didn't let go. "How do you handle civil disobedience?"

"Civil disobedience?"

"You know, when people don't obey you. They break the law by doing a nonviolent sit-in for a cause or something like that."

Rolf shrugged. "As long as they're civil, so am I."

"Do you still call them 'sir' or 'ma'am'?"

Rolf shrugged.

"Even if they disobey you?"

"As long as they're civil," Rolf said, with an air of finality, to signal those were his final words on the subject.

Gus said, "What I don't get is, why does all disobedience have to be civil? It isn't fair."

Sylvia darted a sharp glare at Gus, who grinned back at her through his thick black beard.

To Rolf, Sylvia said, "Anyway, we're all friends at the Madhouse. You don't need to call Gus 'sir' here."

"Get used to it, Sylvia," Hack said. "Cops call everyone sir."

"Even when they're arresting you?" Sylvia asked.

"Especially when they're arresting you," Gus said. He turned to Hack. "What's up with you, Partner?"

"What do you mean?" Hack said.

"Those were the first words you said all night. Usually, we can't shut you up."

"I've been thinking," Hack said.

"Uh oh," Gus said.

Mattie patted Hack's arm. "He does that from time to time. But it will pass. It always does."

Hack mustered a smile as weak as her joke.

"It's like the Theseus paradox," Debra said out of nowhere.

142

"What?" Her husband Rolf asked.

"The Theseus paradox," Debra said. "You know."

Everyone but Hack and Sylvia shook their heads as if they didn't know, Hack because he was only half-listening, Sylvia because, whatever the topic, she always acted as if she did know, which the others tolerated because she usually did.

Sylvia asked, "Debra, how do you know about the Theseus paradox?"

Sylvia was Professor of Literature at the College. This made her relationship with Gus the most unlikely pairing since world-famous author Arthur Miller paired off with Marilyn Monroe. In this duo, Gus was the big hairy Marilyn.

"LG told me," Debra said.

"LG?" Sylvia said, "What did he say?"

Mattie asked, "Sylvia, have you met Gus's son LG yet?"

"Only briefly," Sylvia said.

"You're in for a treat," Mattie said. "He's a genius. Gus, what's LG up to these days?"

"I'm not sure," Gus said. "He doesn't tell me much. It's almost like he's not the same kid."

"That's my point," Debra said. "According to the Theseus paradox, maybe he isn't."

"Okay, Debra," Rolf said to his wife. "Tell everybody about the article LG told you to read."

"Okay," Debra said. "In ancient Greek times, a hero named Theseus sailed off to adventure. His ship got broken up. He had to fix it up with all new parts. Naturally, the question came up, with all those new parts, was it still the same ship?"

"Naturally," Rolf said.

"Like Hack's 1973 Audi Fox," Gus said.

"What's the connection?" Sylvia asked him.

"I rebuilt the thing pretty much from scratch," Gus said. "I used almost all replacement parts."

"So maybe it's not the same car as it was?" Sylvia asked.

"According to Debra and her paradox, I guess," Gus said.

Sylvia asked, "So how does this connect with LG?"

"Well," Debra said, "I also read that all the cells in our bodies get replaced every seven years."

Gus asked, "If all his cells got replaced, then LG really isn't the same person he was seven years ago?

"Exactly," Debra said.

Gus said, "That would explain a lot." He took a swig of beer. He asked, "And all our cells get replaced every seven years?"

Debra nodded again.

"And that goes for everyone, including me?" Gus asked. He set his bottle down on the table and shook his head. "Actually, it's kind of a relief,"

"Why's that?" Sylvia asked.

"Don't you get it?" Gus said. "I read too, and I heard that the human brain continues to mature for years, all the way to 25."

Sylvia asked, "So you should have to reach 25 to count as an adult?"

"Or drink," Mattie said.

"Or marry," Hack said.

"Or vote," Gus said.

"You don't vote anyway," Sylvia reminded Gus.

Rolf said, "Or drive. Would make the highways safer tonight."

"Now we're really off the subject," Sylvia said.

"No, we're right on top of the subject," Gus said. "It's been more than seven years since I was 25. And maybe I matured and got sharp at age 25, for an hour or two," Gus said. "But right in that tiny instant of peak intelligence, aging kicked in. My deterioration began. Since then, it's been all downhill. Which means I had something like one day in my life when I was in top brain. Maybe only an hour or a minute."

"Based on my experience with men," Mattie said, "Most of them never even have that minute. My guy here is one of the few." She laid her hand gently on the back of Hack's neck. Hack resisted the impulse to wriggle like a puppy.

Sylvia said, "Gus, you've lost me again. What has this got to do with what we're talking about?"

Gus said, "It's been more than seven years since I was 25. If I'm not the same person, I'm off the hook for every stupid thing I did before that. Like in my teens and early twenties. I just wasn't fully matured yet."

"And now?" Sylvia asked.

Rolf said, "This theory would explain what Debra and I see every day on the job. Young idiots doing stupid things." He shook his head. "Sometimes terrible things."

Debra said, "And if young men's brains haven't matured yet, maybe that's why there are so many fatherless children."

"The women who get pregnant by them are just as stupid," Mattie said. "Those children aren't cloned."

"Sometimes the women are pretty sly," Debra said. "You see all those celebrities and athletes in court with their baby-mamas and the baby-mamas waving their DNA test results in the air like bearer bonds they can turn in for gold."

Mattie said. "In that situation, it's the man who's the fool."

"All too true," Gus said. "A fool and his sperm are soon parted."

13 Laghdaf

Monday morning. "How goes the antislavery crusade?" Hack asked Laghdaf.

"Please don't use that word," Laghdaf said.

"You mean 'slavery'?"

"I mean 'crusade'," Laghdaf said. "We Muslims are not fond of crusades. Jews feel the same way, in case you are wondering."

"I'll keep that in mind," Hack said. "But I'm still asking how it's going."

The two were sitting at a table in Sven's Hot Mug in Ojibwa City, ninety miles from Laghdaf's Minneapolis office. Hack wanted a private conversation, and Laghdaf told Hack he wanted to get out of "this meshugge town," for a few hours anyway.

Laghdaf sipped his green tea and glanced around at the wobbly tables and chairs and the equally wobbly Monday morning customers, restless in line, shuffling their feet, desperate for their caffeine. He said, "Minneapolis has become too crazy for a simple country boy like me. I have always liked Ojibwa City better."

"Ever thought about moving here?" Hack asked.

Laghdaf nodded. "Yes. But it would be a long commute to court."

"I thought court is mostly over the Internet these days."

"Someday things may return to normal."

"And, when they do, you'll be close at hand," Hack said.

"Close at hand, that's where I'll be." Laghdaf sighed, an unusually dour expression on his dark face.

Hack said, "I have a legal issue."

"As I anticipated when I received your call," Laghdaf said.

"Well, several issues, really. First, it happens that I'm holding a sum of money which is not mine."

146

Laghdaf didn't blink. A client holding money not his. What else is new?

Hack said, "Which I'd like to return to its rightful owners."

Laghdaf tilted his head and cocked his left eyebrow, as if to say, now something new.

"But anonymously," Hack said. "And I thought you could suggest something. You know, like a trust account or something like that."

"What would you use this account for?"

"To get people their money back. And it would have to be anonymous, you know, secret. Maybe pretend it's a foundation set up by a reclusive billionaire or something like that."

"Have you been out righting wrongs again?" Laghdaf asked.

Hack shrugged.

Laghdaf said, "It sounds as if you are discussing a large sum of money."

"I don't know for sure."

"How can that be?"

"That's my second issue," Hack said. "I thought you might know something about cryptocurrency."

"Why might I?"

"I had the idea your antislavery crusade or whatever you want to call it has put you in touch with a lot of different people."

Laghdaf nodded. "Many different people and different sorts of people."

Hack and Sam agreed that Laghdaf was the person to ask because Laghdaf's experience made him an expert on the international underworld. Laghdaf had been born a slave in Mauritania. He'd escaped and come to America, and with a typical immigrant's dogged zeal, he had worked his way through law school. Using his newly acquired status as an attorney and, better yet, as law partner to the infamous Sam Lapidos, Laghdaf was doing whatever he could to abolish or at least slow down human trafficking, not only in Africa, but in South America and the U.S.

Hack asked, "Don't some of these human traffickers and drug and arms dealers do business in cryptocurrency?"

"As do many honest people and businesses," Laghdaf said. "Much of the crypto universe is regulated and above-board."

"But some of it is not, right?"

Laghdaf sipped his tea and stared over his cup at Hack, giving no clue what he was thinking. "That statement is also true."

"Which brings me to my third problem. A hypothetical problem, I mean."

"Before you speak more of your hypothetical problem," Laghdaf said. "Please allow me to explain a few realities to you, lawyer to client."

"Okay."

"It is illegal to traffic in stolen property, even if stolen from a thief."

"I know that too," Hack said.

"The word 'traffic' includes conducting any transactions whatsoever, including, hypothetically, returning stolen money to victims."

"Yep." Hack said.

"Excellent," Laghdaf said. "Now, what are the hypothetical questions you want to ask?"

"Hypothetically, what if someone came into possession of cryptocurrency some thieves used to store their loot?"

"Possession?"

Hack nodded.

"Possession is an interesting word to use when talking about cryptocurrency," Laghdaf said. "Like most contemporary money, crypto lacks physical reality. Do you mean this hypothetical someone knows the private password which will enable him to unlock the cryptography and thereby exert control over the currency?"

"Yes," Hack said. "I mean that."

"I can give you only legal advice. And it appears you are already familiar with the legal basics. For technical issues, it seems advisable to refer you to someone else."

"Who?"

"His name is Hatfield McGray," Laghdaf said. "He is an expert on all technical matters having to do with crypto currency and the Internet generally. Laghdaf paused. "And by expert, I mean the genuine thing, not the pretentious clowns who call themselves experts in our degenerating age."

It was true. Laghdaf was way more dour than usual.

Hack asked, "How do I get in touch with him?"

"You don't. But I shall speak with him. He may contact you."

Throughout the conversation, the Hot Mug sound system had been treating its customers to soporific folk guitar, the kind of quiet music over which customers find it easy to ramble on about their favorite topic, themselves.

Out of nowhere the system went into an eccentric distracting tune which tugged like a hungry cat, claws poking through the fabric of your shirt sleeve, demanding immediate attention.

Laghdaf smiled and leaned back. "Ah, *Brilliant Corners*. Thelonious Monk. A pleasant surprise."

"Sven must have arrived," Hack said. "Taken over from his teenage baristas and changed the music."

"I knew I liked this coffee shop."

"There's more to Sven than meets the eye," Hack said.

Laghdaf glanced over at the counter. "Is that him?"

Behind the counter, an older white man with shaggy gray-blonde hair and an even shaggier beard was making a sandwich. He wore a sweatshirt with the sleeves cut off and no hair net.

"Could be," Hack said. "I'm not sure what Sven looks like myself."

"You said, 'meets the eye'," Laghdaf reminded Hack.

"Yes, I did," Hack said. "You know Thelonious Monk music?"

"Yes, and Sonny Rollins too," Laghdaf said. "He plays saxophone on that track."

"I know," Hack felt compelled to say, if only to show Laghdaf that he knew too.

Laghdaf relaxed his normally erect posture and leaned back in his chair. "Thelonious Monk is the reason I met Sam."

"That I didn't know," Hack said.

Laghdaf asked, "How did you think Sam and I first met?"

"I never thought about it at all," Hack said. "For a while, Sam was my father-in-law. Then my wife Lily convinced a court she wasn't my wife anymore, so he wasn't my father-in-law anymore either, just my lawyer and friend. And you, at first you weren't there and then you were. You kind of popped into existence."

"Yes, I am known for my popping," Laghdaf's radiant smile burst across his face, spilling light in every direction. "Sam and I met at a jazz club. Fine local musicians did a scintillating performance, entirely Monk tunes. Hard music to play, I suspect, with all those odd rhythms and harmonies."

"You suspect right."

Laghdaf said, "Sam was there too. The place was jammed. The only empty seat was at my table. He joined me. We fell into conversation. He learned I was studying the law, and the rest is history, as is said."

"Monk music was all it took?"

"We also happened to meet again later, at a performance of Henry Wadsworth music. Even harder to play, I suppose."

"Right again. And you talked with him that time too?"

"There was no one else to talk with. The audience was just the two of us and a lovely young lady we surmised was Henry Wadsworth's girlfriend of the moment."

"Henry has never drawn big crowds," Hack said.

"And he never will," Laghdaf said.

14 Hatfield McGray

In his brief Monday phone call to Hack, Hatfield McGray
told Hack he'd be glad to explain all things crypto, but only if
Hack met him at Hatfield's own Minneapolis home.

Tuesday morning, after Hack checked out the address, he
recognized the neighborhood Hatfield lived in.

Hack had a current Minnesota Conceal Carry permit. He
took his souvenir Arizona holster and revolver out of his gun
safe and laid them on the kitchen table and thought about
whether he should carry them along.

Deciding that even the most desperate carjacker would
snub Hack's little red 1973 Audi Fox, Hack locked the revolver
in the safe again.

Hack drove his Fox the ninety minutes to Minneapolis.
Once in Minneapolis, Hack's route took him down a main
thoroughfare past the detritus of riot destruction—burned out
restaurants, black skeletons of dead gas stations, a forlorn
locksmith shop with broken windows and an intact door, three
abandoned groceterias, a huge barren Waldo with an empty
parking lot, and squads of useless looking men loitering in
bunches on the streets with nothing legal to do.

Some of the men were obviously selling drugs. More
depressing, some had been buying. They now drooped half-
conscious against the sides of the broken buildings.

Minneapolis had once been a decent place to live. Now it
was looking like every other big city.

For the moment though, no gunfire, which was comforting.

Hatfield Gray greeted Hack at his front door and let Hack
in. He led Hack through the house to his roofed but open back
porch. The two sat on blond wicker chairs which faced out to a
weedy back yard. Hatfield had set a pitcher of coffee on a
small table between the chairs. Hatfield poured Hack some

coffee in a standard mug. He chugged his own coffee from a red clay mug the size and shape of a small flowerpot. It had no handle, so maybe it was a flowerpot.

Raised white letters on it proclaimed, *"**Nobody Does it Like Money.**"*

Hatfield was a tallish bearded dude in his twenties with a contemporary haircut—high dark brush on top, shaved near bald on the sides. His ripped biceps and triceps bulged beneath the long sleeves of his pink tee shirt. Emblazoned in black on the front of the shirt were the words, *"**DIGITAL MONEY.**"*

Hatfield's coffee was excellent. For a few moments Hack sat with Hatfield in comfortable silence, enjoying the coffee and the unusually warm late autumn day, until, with no warning, Hatfield leaned towards Hack and asked him, "What is money?"

"I'm not sure," Hack said.

"Where does it come from?"

"Money's just always been there. I've never thought much about it."

"It's time you do think about it," Hatfield said. "It's time everyone thinks about it. Because what everyone calls money isn't."

"Isn't what?"

Hatfield raised his flowerpot in two hands and chugged from it and set it back in his lap. His eyes seemed to bulge out from beneath his thick black brows. Maybe from zeal, maybe from the massive dose of caffeine, maybe from his everyday personality. "Isn't money."

"Then what is it?"

"Cash is trash. It's fake. It's fiat." He shot out his words in a rapid staccato. He sneered out the word "fiat" as if the word were another four-letter obscenity he regretted letting pass his lips.

"Fiat? You mean like the Italian car?"

"Exactly!" Hatfield jumped up and began to pace back and forth, a professor enraptured by his own lecture. As he paced, his bare feet thumped in time with his words on the floor. His big toe was a tom-tom slapping the wood.

He declared, "You know, like in the Bible, the Lord declares, *'Fiat lux',* which is Latin for 'let there be light'."

He raised his hands towards heaven and shouted, "And our Lords and Masters the governments and banks declare, 'Fiat Money', saying 'Let there be money', and there's money out of nowhere, representing nothing. And we accept this fiat money like it's real, real like gold or silver, which it isn't, at least not since Nixon took the dollar off the gold standard back in 1973."

He stopped and pointed an accusing finger at Hack. "You accept the fiat, don't you?"

"I do," Hack admitted. "I accept the fiat."

"Don't feel bad. I accept the fiat too. We all accept it. We're captives, riding in the back seat of a rusty little Italian sportster, headed wherever the lunatic driver wants to take us. So back to my first question. If money's not fiat, what is it?"

"You tell me."

"Money serves three functions," Hatfield said. He lifted the index finger of his right hand. "First, it's a store of value, to save up and invest for the future."

He lifted two fingers. "Second, it's a measure of value, useful in accounting, to keep track of what things are worth, you know, like the buildings and equipment your boss owns."

He lifted three fingers. "Third, it's a means of exchange. We use it to buy and sell things. Do you understand what I'm saying?"

"So far. Three functions. Money."

"If the government can just issue money to do all these things, why can't the rest of us?"

Hack answered, "I guess it's because the government forces people to use its money. It's the law. It says right on the paper dollar, 'legal tender for all debts public and private'."

"The government," Hatfield said. "Who says the government is God?"

"Good question," Hack said. Actually, it was a good question. Hack added, "Not me, that's for sure."

Hatfield cocked his head and spread his hands like a diplomat. "Maybe a better comparison is with old time colonialism."

"Colonialism?"

"Our government in faraway DC operates with the mentality of a hostile occupying foreign power."

"It does?"

"Like 19th century imperialists in Africa," Hatfield said. "Our rulers and their supporters see themselves as our civilizers. DC is their Kinshasa. We're the natives out in the Belgian Congo jungle, the ignorant naked heathen savages it's their religious duty to civilize."

Of course, back in colonial times, Congo people wore clothes and lived in villages, but why break the man's flow?

Hatfield must have guessed Hack's thought. "I'm not saying that about Africa myself. I'm saying that's how DC thinks of us. And our will—us natives and our will to resist—must be broken. That's why all the anti-racism brainwashing and why they want to chop the dicks off little boys and all the rest. If they can make us agree to things we know aren't true, they can also make us pretend their fake money is real, and they stay rich and powerful while we stay poor and powerless."

Hack said nothing. Carried forward by his fervor, Hatfield went on. "The Russia hoax, January 6 hysteria, the whipped-up pandemic hysteria and all the climate change scams and boondoggles are just tools to enhance the power of our rulers, like the social Darwinism, the racism and the genocidal wars of their colonialist predecessors."

Hack asked, "What has cryptocurrency got to do with all this?"

"Crypto is the most potent resistance tool we've ever had. It bypasses all the institutions of power. A world in which crypto is the currency is a world without Big Banks, without Big Government, without Big Tech. We conduct the entire economy without our overlords and their hold over us fades away."

"Fades away? Like the state is supposed to fade away under communism?"

No communist state had ever faded away, anywhere, anytime.

Hatfield ignored the question. He raised his two fists towards heaven in defiance. "We must resist. I resist. They won't break my will. We won't let them dictate to us. We decide what is money."

"Thank you for the explanation," Hack said. "You're giving me much to think about, so much more than I anticipated. I've been reading up on cryptocurrency myself, and I have this question."

Hatfield stared into Hack's eyes. He said, "Spring it, Dawg."

"You called money a means of exchange," Hack said. "To buy things with, right? Goods and services?"

"Yes."

"But does crypto do that? What if you go to the store and try to exchange some of my crypto for a dozen eggs and they refuse? Is the crypto still money?"

"It is if they take it." Hatfield said.

"But if they don't? If no one takes your crypto, it's not a means of exchange, is it?"

"I suppose not," Hatfield said. "For right now."

"Right now I don't think most merchants are taking crypto," Hack said. "And you said money stores value. How does my crypto store value now if I can't buy anything with it later?"

Hatfield shrugged. "There's always a what-if. And how is that different from the little pieces of paper in your wallet or the numbers on the screen in your bank account, losing value every single day? What if, after a few more years of inflation, no one will take them? What if DC keeps manufacturing its fiat currency which gets worth less and less every day until it takes a million dollars to buy a sandwich?"

Another good question.

Hatfield sat back down. He took a sip from his flowerpot. The evangelism faded. As his face relaxed its tension, he shed ten years. Even his scalp unclenched its intense grip on his top knot, which settled lower and flatter on his head. "But enough about me. Why are you here?"

"I don't know what Laghdaf told you."

"He told me I should trust you and I should help you."

"That's all?"

"That's enough." Hatfield folded his hands in his lap and waited, transformed from feverish missionary to sweet Buddha, quiet and composed, half-smiling, eyes kind and accepting, his entire inner world at peace.

Hack said, "I have the private key to decrypt some cryptocurrency. I have reason to believe I'm the only one with that key. I think that makes it mine."

"Okay. Which crypto is it? There are hundreds."

Hack said, "I never heard of it. I've looked on the Internet, and it's not listed on any exchange I've found."

"Does it have a name?"

"Yes, in what I think is Bengali, which I don't read."

"Show me." Hatfield stood.

15 The Redemption

Hack followed as Hatfield led him indoors into the kitchen.

Hack stopped by the tiny brown kitchen table. "More coffee?" he asked.

"No thanks."

"Just me, I guess," Hatfield said. He emptied a the few dregs from his flowerpot mug into the sink and refilled his clay pot from the spigot of a commercial-sized aluminum-sided coffeemaker shining high and tall on the counter.

It was huge. Maybe Hatfield had bought it secondhand from the kitchen of the St. Paul Hotel.

They sat on hard wooden chairs at the table. Hatfield chugged some coffee and put his pot down on the tabletop and folded his hands. All was calm.

Hack took his laptop out of its case and booted it and set the case on the linoleum floor under the table.

Hack asked, "What's your Wi-Fi password?"

"We won't use Wi-Fi here," Hatfield said. "Too hackable. You have an ethernet port on that laptop, don't you?"

"Of course," Hack said. He reached down into his case and pulled out his 12-foot ethernet cable. He looked around and spotted a port in the wall next to the one of the outlets. He plugged one end of the cable into the wall port and the other end into his laptop. He trusted his guess that the entire house was hack-proofed.

He opened the file containing the hacked crypto currency's private key and swiveled it so Hatfield could see the screen.

"Twelve words," Hack said. "Or maybe twelve chunks of characters grouped together like words."

ঘোড়া

কুকুর

গাছ
আকাশ
মন্দির
পশু
লাল
নরম
লম্বা
প্রাচীন
চালানোর
জন্য
বিড়াল

"Is that Hindi?" Hatfield asked.

"No, it's Bengali," Hack said. "I checked it out. Maybe to us Americans, the two scripts look identical, but they're slightly different."

"And you've got no idea what any of that means?"

"None."

"It doesn't matter, you know." Hatfield said.

"Really?"

"They're random anyway. Even if you could read that alphabet, those strings of letters would have no meaning we care about. You just need them so that at the right time you can copy and paste them in the right order into the right place on a computer screen."

Hack looked at Hatfield. "When and where?"

"Type what I tell you and we'll find out," Hatfield said.

Hack did. Under Hatfield's direction, he entered the Darknet.

"Darknet" is a generic term for a vast array of network services, in part a cyberspace underworld used by drug and human traffickers and terrorists, and in part a refuge for private communications. some even legitimate. It is the bulk of the Internet iceberg, underwater and therefore unseen above the surface.

The Darknet lumps together secret bazaars for drug and weapon transactions, human trafficking sites, private friend-to-friend networks, private file transfer services, anonymous political and religious discussion groups, and sexually oriented territories whose denizens prize anonymity almost above life.

The Darknet is a jungle, and not the kindly kind some euphemize as "rain forest." In some of Hack's work for Sam, Hack had macheted his way around it. but Hack was only a dude tourist.

If Laghdaf was correct, Hatfield was the sure-handed guide who could lead Hack past landmarks and signposts and down trails visible only to himself.

Thirty minutes later, a Darknet website home page stared out of Hack's screen:

CryptoWarren

Watch Your Crypto Multiply Like Bunnies!
No Fees
No Custody Solution

"An over-the-counter dealer," Hatfield explained. "OTC."

"Like with stocks?"

"Exactly like," Hatfield said. "Just like there's stock exchanges and over-the-counter stock dealers, there's crypto exchanges and OTC crypto dealers. In an exchange, the middleman takes a cut. Over the counter, there's no middleman. The seller and buyer deal direct. And that's you, right? A seller looking for a buyer?"

"True."

"And I've dealt with this particular dealer. They won't scam you."

Would Hatfield scam him? But Laghdaf recommended Hatfield and Hack trusted Laghdaf with his life. Nothing Hack could do about it anyway.

Hatfield added, "And they will recognize and deal in your particular crypto."

"How do you know that?"

"They know their business," Hatfield said.

"What does that phrase on the website mean, 'No custody solution'?"

"Your only proof of your ownership of any crypto is what they call your custody, which means your knowing the private password to decrypt it. If you lose track of your password—your private key—to any crypto you buy, you've lost that crypto forever. They're warning you that custody of your private key is your problem—not theirs. The risk is all on you."

"But I'm selling," Hack said. "Any problem with holding on to the key is the buyer's, right?"

"Right." Hatfield said. "Once you sell."

"What now?" Hack asked

"What fiat currency do you want to be paid in?"

"U.S. Dollars."

"Do you have Internet access to an account to put those dollars into?'

"Yes."

"Here's what you do." Hatfield guided Hack through the process of offering the crypto for sale.

Hack received three offers in the first few minutes:

$192,014.27
$211,246.13
$182,474.21

"What's going on?" Hack asked. "These are all so different."

"Crypto is volatile," Hatfield said. "Its value fluctuates all the time."

"This fast?"

"Not usually," Hatfield said, "I guess yours fluctuates more quickly than some others."

"Why?"

Hatfield said, "No profit in guessing."

"What do I do?"

"I guess wait for an offer you really like and grab it while you can," Hatfield said.

"You guess?"

Hatfield asked, "More coffee?"

"No thanks.'

Hatfield got up and poured his old coffee into the sink and drew another flowerpot-full out of the spigot of his giant coffee maker. He sat again and took another belt. Considering his consumption, he seemed less jittery than he should have been.

Maybe he was the caffeine version of one of those drunks who can guzzle a fifth of whisky and bowl three perfect frames in a row.

Hack said, "I'm a little concerned about one thing."

"What's that?"

"I'd like to make it hard as possible to trace the money back to me."

"I see." Hatfield nodded.

Hatfield seemed content to let the silence sit between them, forcing Hack to ask, "Is there a way to make sure of that?"

"Sure. For example, you can do a peel chain."

"What's that?"

"An owner pipes his crypto through a chain of very small transactions across very large number of exchanges. Makes it harder to trace."

"Does that work?"

Hatfield nodded. "It can. But the process can nibble away the value, you know, what with all these third party's biting off little chunks in transaction fees and the like."

"Sounds complicated."

"It can be. But the process can be automated with software to speed it up. Hundreds or even thousands of transactions can happen at light speed."

"I wouldn't know where to start to code that."

"You're in luck," Hatfield said, "I've already coded the entire process. I can take care of it. You just tell me where to put the dollars at the end of the chain."

"That'd be perfect," Hack said.

"I get a fee, though."

"How much?"

"Depends," Hatfield said.

"I don't care, actually," Hack said. "I just need enough cash in dollars to pass on to people. So they can get their stolen money back."

Hatfield gave him a speculative look. "A do-gooder, huh?"

"Not likely," Hack said.

"It's okay," Hatfield said. "Even do-gooders do a little good now and then. But how much do you need?"

"$200,000 should do it," Hack said.

"Tell you what," Hatfield said. "I'll make sure that after all the fees, including mine, you'll wind up with exactly $200,000."

"That sounds fair," Hack said.

"I got expenses."

"Of course," Hack said.

"And all this expertise took a lot of time and effort to earn."

"Of course," Hack said.

"Expertise like mine doesn't come cheap."

"I already agreed," Hack said. One more question nagged him. "If crypto is money, why do I need to turn it into government fiat money?"

Hatfield shrugged. "For the time being, government money is more widely accepted in daily life, like in restaurants, mortgage payments, rent, grocery stores, and so on. For the time being, government money is the means of exchange. For the time being, it's what almost everyone wants."

"For the time being?"

Hatfield nodded. "For the time being."

Hack could have asked Hatfield how long that time was going to keep on being, or if it would ever stop being, but Hack didn't bother. No way Hatfield McGray or anyone else could know.

This entire cryptocurrency thing seemed like a wild bet on an unknown future.

Hack said, "There is one more thing. It has nothing to do with the crypto."

"Okay."

"One of the victims of this scam is a man named Henry Wadsworth. I knew a man by that name once, but it's a pretty common name. I'm wondering if you can help me find out if it's the same guy."

Hatfield asked, "Can't you do it yourself?"

"I am working on it myself, but it won't hurt to have someone with your skills also taking a look. I'll pay extra for your time."

Hatfield studied Hack a few moments. Then, "This do-gooding thing must be contagious. Tell you what. Give me what you know about this dude, and we'll see. If I can do it quick and dirty, I won't charge a dime more than the commission I'm already taking."

16 Carole Lager

Hack was sitting in his living room easy chair, dandling a giggling Sammy on his knee, with Mattie humming in the kitchen nearby as she cooked up a dinner suited to a grizzly fresh out of hibernation.

She'd already fed Sammy her own way. Hack had never seen Mattie happier than when she was breast feeding Sammy.

Would Sammy appreciate all the love Mattie and Hack were lavishing on him?

Who knew?

Did Sarai? At twelve, she was getting more independent every day, but still seemed loving, though of course gratitude was in short supply.

Had Hack been as grateful as he ought to have been to his own mom and dad?

Not even close, and too late now.

Anyway, Hack didn't need gratitude from Sarai. For gratitude, he could get a dog. A lot of old people had dogs. Probably the reason.

What about gratitude towards Henry Wadsworth?

Any time Hack's fingers touched a music keyboard, like at the Madhouse, no matter how much fun he was having, no matter how the people around seemed to enjoy the music he was helping to make, he felt a small but relentless sense of failure. Was he really bringing his best?

Every time he asked himself that question he thought of Henry.

There had been no breakup, if that was the right word. There was no definite moment the sessions ended. He'd never even called Henry and said goodbye.

Hack had acted something like all the self-absorbed punks who later shunned Hack at GC when he'd become toxic, after he'd been labeled a purveyor of sexism and racism and all the other isms, when only Cal would be seen with him, because Cal himself had gone crazy.

Why'd he ducked out on Henry?

Fear? Because he feared plunging himself down into the obvious pit of isolation and impotence in which Henry had buried himself?

Embarrassment? Because he was failing to live up to all the effort Henry had put into teaching him?

Youthful self-absorption? He'd just gone on to the next phase of his own life, as if Henry Wadsworth was some kind of extra in the private movie which played in Hack's head, the story Hack was starring in?

He'd been thoughtless and heedless and feckless—all the lesses. He'd been too absorbed in his own feelings and his own misadventures to remember that Henry also had feelings and misadventures.

Sure, he could rationalize: since his sessions with Henry, Hack had been simplifying his music, getting down to basics, honing his music down to the fundamental chords and rhythms and melodies of America, the country, western, rock, R&B, the stuff they called "roots music."

On the surface that sounded like a semi-decent excuse, but to be more honest, what it came down to was that Hack was a jerk.

And what about his first teacher Ms. Lager—where was she now?

Hack picked up Sammy and set him straddling Hack's hip and walked into the kitchen. Sammy bent from Hack's hip and grunted and reached out with both hands for his mother. She kissed his cheek and went back to stirring chunks of meat and vegetables in a red sauce, in an aluminum pot about the circumference of a backyard plastic swimming pool, but deeper.

She narrowed her eyes at Hack. "What are you two doing in here?" Mattie didn't like distractions when cooking.

"Just a question."

"Make it quick, please. I'm about to do the hard part."

"You remember Carole Lager?"

"The piano teacher?"

"My piano teacher," Hack reminded her.

"Of course. What about her?"

"Do you know what happened to her?"

Mattie kept stirring and stared at the wall as if thinking it over. "Yeah. I do. She met a nice lady gym teacher and moved in with her and then they moved to St Paul."

"What gym teacher? You mean Ms. Naby?"

"Yes."

"Didn't everyone say Ms. Naby was a lesbian?"

"Not without reason," Mattie said.

"Ms. Lager is a lesbian too?"

"You didn't know that?"

"I never thought about it."

Mattie shook her head. "Do you ever notice anyone else?" Her expression softened. "Sorry. I know that's not fair. You were just a teenager back then, and only bright about a few things."

After eating his dinner and recovering and helping Mattie put Sammy to bed, Hack seated himself in front of his laptop and searched for Carole Lager's number—of course, using his own homemade search engine USearchIT instead of the ones he hated, like Google or PrivaNation.

He dialed the number he found for her

"Hello?" A nice alto. Ms. Lager's voice for sure.

"Hi, Ms. Lager. I don't know if you remember me, but this is Hack Wilder. I mean Nate. You gave me piano lessons." Which name had she used for him?

"Of course I remember you, Hack. How are you?"

"I'm fine. And you?"

"Just fine too," she said. "It's lovely to hear your voice. Is there something I can do for you?"

"Nothing. I just wanted to thank you. For the teaching and everything."

"That's very nice. And unusual, too. Thanks for thinking of me."

"Are you still giving lessons?"

"No," she said. "I'm retired now."

"And Ms. Naby?"

"Ms. Naby is great. Would you like to speak with her?"

"No, that's not necessary."

"As you wish," she said. "Is there anything else?"

"No, that's it. Thank you, is all."

"And thank you, too, Hack. You were a wonderful student." She hung up.

Hack hung up too.

Mattie was standing nearby, giving him a wifely once-over. She asked, "Is this like one of those twelve-step programs? Where you have to visit and apologize to everyone you've ever done wrong?"

"No," Hack said. "It's just two steps."

17 Benedetto

Hack's old college roommate Bennett might know something about what happened to Henry. Bennett had stayed around Chicago for several years after graduation. Besides, it was time to catch up.

Bennett had suffered a frustrating first year after graduation. He couldn't get a gig. A hundred or more flute players auditioned for every one of the few symphonic openings in North America.

Desperate, Bennett switched from classical concert flute to pan flute. Instead of the single long tube of a concert flute, the pan flute was triangle shaped.

According to legend, the ancient Greek god Pan invented the pan flute. The god set different-length reeds together in a row and bound them into the triangle.

With his new authentic old instrument, Bennett started busking outside downtown theaters and concert halls, his fedora open on the ground for donations. He was skillful enough to start taking in cash.

Encouraged by the sudden influx of money, he polished his act. He took on his original Greek family name, "Benedetto." He dyed his red hair to black and grew it down to his shoulders and curled it in the ancient Athenian fashion. In performance, he wore a long white tunic, a sort of knee-length tee shirt made of wool or linen, tied with a belt at the waist.

Bennett didn't just stand and toot like a classical concert performer. Always nimble and agile, he incorporated into his act a kind of glide, full of small goat-like hops. He could play and dance at the same time.

Bennett took his startup busking cash and invested in recording pop melodies over a smooth synthesized background. He began selling recordings at booths he set up at malls and fairs. He called his first recording *Strains of Arcadia* after the legendary Greek district home of Pan. Then he branched out with recordings of country tunes. As his income grew, so did the ensembles he recorded with.

Next thing Hack knew, Benedetto was an international presence. Hack had seen some of the Internet videos, shot at packed concerts with genuine full orchestras, at the Acropolis in Greece, the Sphinx in Egypt, and New York City's Central Park.

Tens of thousands assembled to watch Benedetto play his pan flute and dance across the stage.

Hack didn't begrudge his friend the fame or the money. All musicians are underpaid. Bennett had a wife and four children.

Hack and Bennett had kept in occasional touch. Hack texted him. "Bennett—Got a few minutes?"

Five minutes later the answering text came back. "No problem. Video chat? But give me thirty minutes to close out a licensing deal."

"Sure," Hack texted back. He seated himself before his computer with Sammy in his lap and emailed Bennett the video chat link.

Lately Sammy had been trying to help Hack type. Hack had given him a tiny fake keyboard to use while Hack used the real thing. Sammy ignored it, preferring to type on Hack's real thing. Most of the time, Hack let him.

Hack gave Bennett an hour, during which he amused himself by checking out Benedetto's more recent music videos, hits like *Crystal Vortex, Vortex of Crystals, Quarts of Quartz,* and his two biggest hits, *Crystal Meth(anol) Express* and *To The Vectors Belong the Spoils.*

Bennett must have studied hard with a great choreographer. In every video, he performed intricate maneuvers with grace and precision, sometimes in ensembles of a dozen or more dancers.

Benedetto had also taken to wearing his tunic only over one shoulder. He'd bulked up on weights. On the videos, his newly developed biceps and triceps bulged almost as big as his bank account.

Next thing, Bennett and Hack were grinning at each other in their screens.

Bennett's computer camera must have been wide screen. He was lounging on a big deck cushion outdoors on a natural wood deck. Behind the deck's rails were a beach and the blue expanse of the Pacific Ocean.

Malibu.

Bennett wore jean shorts and a white tee shirt. A redhaired baby was crawling across his lap. Two golden retrievers squatted next to him, one on each side, resembling the twin guardian lions of ancient Greek gates, except they were just big drooling dogs.

Hack asked, "How are things in 'Athens By The Sea'?"

"Great. Meet little Plato." Bennett held up his baby, about nine months old. Plato waved his arms and smiled.

"Hello, Plato," Hack said. "Meet Sammy." He held up Sammy. Sammy waved his arms and drooled.

Hack lowered Sammy into his lap again. He'd wipe up the spit later.

"Beautiful," Bennett said.

"Likewise."

"How many you got?"

"Just Sarai—you know about her—and Sammy here. Obviously, he's new. How are your four?"

"Six," Bennett corrected. "I'm still gaining on you."

"All credit to you," Hack said. "But doesn't your plan to populate the earth with little redheads alienate your fan base? I thought they were all green people, the kind who hate human procreation."

"They forgive me," Bennett said. "The ones who know."

"Does Amara ever get tired of birthing all these babies?"

"She loves it. Has something special come up?"

"Yes," Hack said, "I have a question."

"Go ahead."

170

"It's about Henry Wadsworth."

"Your piano teacher back in school? The guy they fired?"

"Yes," Hack said. "But I've lost track of him. You stayed in Chicago a while after I left. Do you know what happened to him?"

Bennett tugged at his long curled beard. "Let me think. Any special reason you want to know?"

"Long story."

Bennett said, "I don't think I ever heard of him again after you left Chicago. And I should have. I mean, I was playing all over town for several years. Never even heard his name. Sorry."

Hack said, "Thanks anyway."

"You know who might know something?" Bennett said. "Rob Botman."

"The jazz critic at the Daily American? I don't think I ever met him."

"In Chicago, I ran into him everywhere. He hates my music, but we became personal friends anyway. He wrote me up on his website as a 'sellout'. Like six times. I take the word sellout as a compliment. Proves I have something to sell. Every so often I forward him a glowing review just to stick it to him."

"Maybe you should just send him your bank statement."

"Maybe I will." Bennett grinned. "Anyway, Botman might know something. After all, it was his job, keeping track of jazz musicians."

"Was?"

"The paper downsized and bought him out. Old time newspapers are disappearing. Haven't you noticed? He's retired now, and maybe a little bored. He might be eager to talk. I could give you his number if you like. You can tell him I gave it to you."

"Thanks."

For a few minutes more they talked about money, babies, wives and money. They signed off. Hack changed his tee shirt and changed Sammy and laid Sammy in his crib for his nap.

18 Rob Botman

A few minutes later, Hack received Bennett's text with Rob Botman's number. Hack got himself another cup of coffee and called the number.

Botman answered right away. "Rob Botman here."

"Hello, Mr. Botman, my name is Hack Wilder. Benedetto gave me your number."

"You friends?"

"We were college roommates. I'd like a few minutes of your time, if you don't mind."

"Nothing but time."

Hack said, "It's about my old teacher Henry Wadsworth."

"Hold it. Did you say Hack Wilder? Hey, I think I remember you."

"Are you sure?" Hack asked. "I don't think we ever met."

"But I heard you play," Botman said. "Piano, right? At a jam session. At the Azure Cat. Must be at fifteen or twenty years ago."

"Are you sure? I only played on two tunes."

"It sticks in my mind because Kwame John was making a stink about you playing. I told him I thought you played fine, which you did, by the way. He didn't care about that. He suspected you were a Henry Wadsworth plant or something crazy like that."

"A plant?"

"They were having some kind of music war," Botman said. "It was insane. He hated Henry Wadsworth."

"Do you know why?"

A pause, then, "Why dig up old scores?"

Hack asked, "Do you know what happened to Kwame John?"

"Sure," Bot said. "He got one of those so-called genius grants. Like a million dollars from some foundation run by rich white pinkos. And now he's up there at the University."

"Doing what?"

"He's Chair of the Music Department."

Hack squelched the impulse to blurt, "But he's a scam artist. He can't play!".

"Kwame's a scam artist. Can't play," Botman said. "It's nuts."

"I studied in that music department," Hack said. "At the University."

"You wouldn't recognize it," Botman said. "They knocked down the Beehive—you remember that?"

"I lived in that building for three years."

"They built a brand-new building. Spent millions. They were so proud. When they opened it, they took a bunch of us on a tour. Gave me champagne and hors d'oeuvres."

Hack asked, "What happened to the Beehive pianos?"

"They moved all those old pianos into the new building. All these beat-up old uprights in these clean ultramodern rooms. Sort of creepy."

Hack asked, "What do you think Kwame John can teach the kids? Anything?"

"I know exactly what he's teaching them," Botman said. "At the front of the building they put this big board where students can write things, you know, about their hopes and dreams and aspirations. College stuff."

"Okay."

"And all I saw on this board was cult preaching. Different students phrased it differently, but it was all the same. One wrote how he was going to use music to overthrow the patriarchy. Another had her big plan to decolonize Eurocentric music. A third was going to overthrow white supremacy by using music."

"How?"

"No specifics provided. I don't want to offend you—"

"You're not."

"Not that I care," Botman said. "Now you tell me, what does that have to do with learning to toot out a tune on your saxophone?"

"Nothing," Hack said.

"Gives me the creeps."

"I understand," Hack said.

"Okay, I'm done ranting," Botman said. "There must be a reason you called. What can I do for you?"

"Well, you're right. Henry Wadsworth was my teacher. By the way, I didn't play at Kwame's jam session because I was acting as Henry's plant or anything like that."

"Obviously," Botman said. "Although I could tell right away you were his student. I remember thinking it at the time."

"Really? How?"

"To be polite, let's say, from what to my taste is unnecessary complexity. Even in the few blues choruses you played. Strange, unusual, eccentric, all those words, but there was something compelling about it anyway. And that's Henry all the way."

"I guess," Hack said. "Do you know what happened to him?"

"You lost contact?"

"I'm afraid I did," Hack said.

"I see. Well, I suppose you could start with his wives."

"Wives?"

"Oh yeah. At least four, I think. And a daughter, maybe."

"Do you know how I can reach them?"

"I can find out. It'll take a couple of days. If you like, I'll email you whatever I find."

"I would really appreciate that," Hack said.

"You've piqued my curiosity."

"Thanks," Hack said.

"And call me anytime. I got nothing much to do these days, except write for my blog."

"I'll check that out," Hack said.

"I'm pretty much out of the loop, but I still have a few friends left in the music scene. If you want a gig, I could put in a word for you."

"That's nice of you," Hack said.

"Call me anytime," Botman said. "Anytime. If only to let me know if you find him."

"I will," Hack told the retired man.

19 Hatfield Gray Reports

One month later, Hack was sitting at his basement work bench. Hack had finally worked his way to the bottom of his Troy Gang Victim Spreadsheet. He had only two names to go.

After Hack's fiascos with the esteemed investment advisor Hugh Duffy and the DODO S. Jackson Wendt, he'd decided to do no more phoning, at least if he could avoid it.

Instead, he set up a new virtual machine he called Vince 3. Within it he created an email server. From his email server he piped emails from his imaginary Justice organization I.O.R.R.R.R. through proxy servers around the world to all of the remaining victims.

Without exception, the people who received his emails were thrilled to get their refunds. Few asked any real questions. After all, they were a pre-selected group of eager believers in emails from unknown sources. Given the chance, most would have invested in Bernie Madoff. Probably some of them did.

Hack's reimbursement fund shrank as the refunds flowed out of it. Most of the refund amounts were relatively trivial, small enough to avoid any law enforcement attention, or so he hoped.

Only two of his emails failed to reach their targets. Each came back with a "permanent fatal error," which meant the email address no longer worked. Henry Wadsworth's was one of them.

Hack had addressed the other rejected email to an organization rather than an individual—something called *The Bastion. The Bastion's* refund would be by far the largest. The Troy Gang had scammed them out of $20,000.

Hack looked up *The Bastion* on its website. Its operators claimed to provide "political analysis and reporting free from tribal loyalties or rancorous partisanship."

A little digging showed that despite its self-proclaimed mission, *The Bastion* was just another bunch of hack political operatives. Hack spotted no consistent political principles. They bent to whatever wind was blowing.

They also bundled substantial funds to political candidates who furthered their donors' business enterprises. In exchange, they received the chance to dip into the stream of money as they passed it along—a very profitable business for themselves.

They'd come into their own—to the extent they'd ever achieved an "own," since few voters paid them any attention—with their dogged hatred, slander and obloquy against a U.S. President, which brought them flattering attention from ZNN and the other media which shared *The Bastion's* hatreds and lack of integrity.

The Bastion's primary funder had been billionaire Frederick Sauer, the same Gogol-Checkov CEO who had driven the successful effort to boot Hack out of what had become Sauer's company.

Later, Hack knew, Sauer had gone broke. In his greed, he'd extended his business enterprises into partnerships with the Chinese Communists. When he failed to satisfy their own boundless greed, they'd smacked his rickety empire down out of spite.

Hack smiled to himself at the memory of his own small personal role in siccing the Chinese Communists on Sauer, and of Sauer's subsequent financial destruction.

True reckonings are rare. Hack had owed Sauer big time, and for once in his life, he'd collected.

From the timing of the Troy Gang fraud, Hack guessed a connection between Sauer's downfall and *The Bastion's* suckerdom. Maybe *The Bastion* had been desperate for funding after their chief sugar daddy had stopped sweetening their pot. Afterwards, their recklessness could have made them vulnerable.

All speculation, but fun speculation.

The Bastion's guru was a well-known pundit named Edward Crunk. Crunk posed as some kind of even-handed moderate who held himself above the various partisan frays and called things as he saw them.

But when the media had ignited a firestorm of hatred towards Hack, falsely accusing Hack of murdering his Muslim friend Amir Mohammed, Crunk had materialized on ZNN to plug into the chorus of slander against Hack—like all the rest, he'd called Hack an "Islamophobic killer."

Crunk was even named in the Hack's defamation lawsuit against ZNN, now emboweled somewhere deep in the multi-intestined American legal system.

Did Hack really want to refund this scuzbucket's money?

Laghdaf was taking the lead on Hack's lawsuit against ZNN. He'd cautioned Hack not to contact ZNN or any other parties or witnesses.

Let *The Bastion* and Edward Crunk stew in their own stupidity.

Hack could make better use of his time looking for Henry, assuming this final Troy Gang victim was Hack's Henry Wadsworth.

Sammy cried out from his crib upstairs in the bedroom. Mattie was at work. Hack had a chance to spend some alone time with his son.

Hack bolted upstairs and into their bedroom. Sammy had pulled himself upright and was leaning against the side of his crib, snuffling. The sight of Hack started a few guilt-inducing tears trickling down his cheeks. He'd already learned to play his parents.

Hack lifted Sammy and sniffed. He carried Sammy into the bathroom and changed his diapers. It was all too obvious Sammy also needed a bath.

Hack partially filled the tub and placed Sammy upright in the shallow water. Hack set out bathing him with a washrag from outside the tub. Sammy was the greatest bath toy ever. He loved sitting in the water and he loved slapping it. Every time Hack slapped and splashed water onto Sammy, he shrieked with laughter and slapped back.

Sammy's games were not sophisticated.

By the time the bath was over, Hack had to dry off both Sammy and himself.

Hack carried Sammy to the bedroom and dressed him.

Just as he finished, Hack's phone rang from the living room.

Hack carried Sammy out to the living room and placed Sammy in his playpen and answered the phone.

It was Hatfield McGray. Hatfield said, "You recall you asked me to check out your man Henry Wadsworth?"

"Of course," Hack said. "You got something?"

"Sort of," Hatfield said.

Hack took a seat in his easy chair, ear to his phone, eyes on Sammy.

Sammy sat upright on the floor of his playpen. For the first time, he stared at the set of seven stacking cups Mattie had put there along with a lot of other toys, as if finally getting around to wondering what the cups were for.

"I found a lot of information on the Henry Wadsworth who must have been your teacher," Hatfield said. "But I don't know yet if he's the same guy who got scammed."

"But that's good already," Hack said. "Thanks."

"I do know he's not dead," Hatfield said.

"How do you know that?"

"The Social Security Administration keeps a public database of people who've died. There's a fair number of Henry Wadsworths there, but none of them matches your guy."

Sammy picked up the beige stacking cup in his right hand.

Hatfield said, "Back in the sixties he used to be a bigshot in among the radicals. Like a Marxist revolutionary. He was something like the official musician for a black nationalist group, but something happened—I can't tell what—and they dumped him, or he dumped them."

Sammy picked up the black beige stacking cup in his left hand. He stared at his two cups. He slapped them together and laughed at the clacking sound. He slapped them together and laughed again.

Hatfield said, "He lived in France awhile. He met an African-French woman and married her. He came back to the U.S. They got divorced and she went back to France."

"How do you know all this?"

"It was in an article about forty years ago. The magazine it appeared in is defunct now. It wasn't around long enough to make it onto the Internet. I'll send you a paper copy if you like."

"Please," Hack said.

Sammy focused his eyes on the two cups in his hands. He twisted them around in his hands, as if fascinated by their colors and shapes He brought them close together again, this time slowly.

Hatfield said, "Some other more recent stuff is on the Internet. I'll send you the links. He was sort of big in the official music world for a while—got a lot of grants. He hasn't got a college degree, but he even had a position for a while as a professor at a university. Then they fired him."

"I know about that part," Hack said.

Sammy was still bringing his two cups together. He twisted them this way and that. Then he changed his plan and held the beige cup in his left hand steady while he brought the black cup in his right hand towards the beige one. His entire face seemed to change with the effort.

Hack had seen that expression before, on the faces of programmers staring at their screens trying to get their code to make sense, or on the faces of musicians laboring to get the intractable instruments in their hands to make good sounds. On the face of everyone trying to do something hard.

"I hope I'm helping you out, Dawg," Hatfield said, "But I'm not sure what you're after."

"You're helping a lot," Hack said. "And I really appreciate the effort."

"By the way, what are you after?" Hatfield asked.

"I owe him. I'm just trying to find the man so I can thank him."

"That's it?"

"Maybe I also don't want the world to forget him the way I forgot him all these years," Hack said.

"I get it," Hatfield said. "You're fighting entropy. But it's a losing battle, Dawg. Forget it."

"What do you mean?"

"Entropy. Time passes. The world winds down, like a clock whose battery's wearing out. Information gets lost. People get forgotten. I barely remember my own grandfather, and I can't tell you anything interesting about my great-grandfather at all, except maybe his name which I got written in the family Bible, which I'm not even sure while I'm talking to you I know where it is. It's the way of the world. Your Henry will be forgotten like almost everybody, like you and me, for that matter. The information will disappear."

"Not necessarily the music, though," Hack said. "Maybe I can save the music."

"What has music got to do with it?"

"Maybe music is information too, and we can save that. See?"

"Not really," Hatfield said. "But it's an interesting idea. I'll check it out."

"You've done more than enough for me," Hack said. "I really appreciate the effort."

"Any time, Dawg," Hatfield said, and hung up.

Sammy took the black cup in his right hand and stuck it into the open top of the larger beige cup in his left hand. It fit. He pulled out the black cup again. He inserted it again. It still fit. He kept doing this with the two cups. Every single time the black cup fit into the beige cup.

Hack followed Sammy's glance as Sammy looked at the other five stacking cups. It was written on Sammy's face: he was making a connection. Sammy bent forward from his sitting position and reached for another cup.

Wow, Hack thought. *Wait till I tell Mattie.*

20 Henry's Family

Rob Botman's email came the next day. Botman provided phone numbers and addresses for two of Henry's wives and one daughter. He wrote, "Sorry—this is the best I could do."

Hack emailed back, "Thanks--it's a great help."

Four wives. Yet Hack didn't recall ever seeing a woman in Henry's apartment. Where'd Henry hidden them? Maybe during those few years Hack had studied with him, Henry had been between wives? Or off women in general? How old had Henry been, anyway?

Mattie was right again. He hadn't been paying attention.

Back at school, Hack had amused himself by coming up with private explanations for Miss Gabor's quirks. But beyond Henry's quirky music, Hack had never even wondered about Henry's.

Henry Wadsworth must have been a fully functioning, breathing, eating, screwing human being. Like the rest of us.

Of course, during that time when Hack studied with Henry, Hack wasn't a fully functioning human being himself. He was just a kid trying to figure out anything he could, which wasn't much.

Hack had been far short of 25, the age the Madhouse crowd agreed you had to reach before you got to vote or drink or get married or drive.

Hack went down to the basement and set himself up at his work bench and called the woman Botman had listed as Delores Wadsworth.

No answer. He left a message with his name and number and why he was calling.

Next he called Shanice Doby, the other wife Botman had identified.

She answered on the third ring. "Hello?"

"Hello, Ms. Doby, my name is Hack Wilder."

"What can I do for you, Mr. Wilder."

"I'm calling about a man named Henry Wadsworth. Many years ago, I used to be his piano student. I'm trying to find him. I've been told you used to be married to him."

"Henry? My Henry?"

"Yes, Ma'am. I guess so."

A low moan. Then weeping. She kept trying to say something, but Hack couldn't understand her words through her sobbing.

Hack said, "Ms. Doby?"

The sobbing intensified.

Hack waited, but her weeping continued until she clicked off the call.

Call her back? No. The decent thing was to leave the woman alone. At least today.

A few hours later, while Hack puttered at tuning his piano—using the same kit Henry had given him—he got a call. He picked up his phone. A woman's voice: "You Hack Wilder?"

"Yes."

"You left a message on my sister's phone?"

"Is your sister Delores Wadsworth?"

"That's her."

"I did call her and leave a message, yes."

"What was your call about?

"Henry Wadsworth," Hack said. "You see, I used to be his student, and—"

"Don't call again." The voice was calm but insistent.

Hack said, "What's that?"

"Please don't call. It will upset her too much."

"I see. May I ask why?"

"You may," the woman said. "But I won't give you any details. It's just all too painful."

"Okay," Hack said. "But do you happen to know where he is?"

"Henry?"

"Yes."

The woman laughed a hard metallic laugh. When she stopped, she said, "You sound like you might be a nice man."

"I try."

"Then do yourself a favor and don't find Henry Wadsworth. But it doesn't matter. I don't know where he is and neither does my sister. And we don't want to. You understand?"

"Yes, I understand," Hack said.

"Fine," she said. "You have a nice day."

"You, too," he said. She hung up. He hung up.

Two down. One to go: Henry's daughter, Henrietta Wadsworth.

Tomorrow was soon enough.

The next morning Hack called Henrietta Wadsworth at the number Botman had given him.

She answered right away. "Hello."

"Hello, Ms. Wadsworth, my name is Hack Wilder."

"Yeah?"

"I'm calling about a man named Henry Wadsworth. I used to be his piano student. I've been told you're his daughter."

"So?"

"Are you Henry's daughter?"

"Maybe."

"I'm trying to find him."

"Why?"

Hack considered trying the old ploy, "To give him money," but figured that lame ruse wouldn't fly, even if this time it wasn't lying. Instead, "A lot of reasons. He was very important in my life."

"Well, he wasn't in mine."

"So you are his daughter?"

185

"Sort of," she said.

"And maybe you know where I can find him?"

"Who you again?"

"Hack Wilder, his former student. Do you know where I can find him?"

"Maybe I do and maybe I don't."

Hack said, "You seem angry at him."

"Listen, that man never did doodley-squat for me. Or my mother. He was supposed to be this great musician and somehow we starved. He left me nothing but that stupid old trunk. He never brought home a dime—that is, when he was home, which I'm glad to say he hardly ever was. I've got nothing to do with him. I want nothing to do with him."

"I see." Hack said.

"Good. Anything else?"

"Did you just say something about a trunk?"

"Maybe I did and maybe I didn't. What about it?"

"Do you know what's in it?"

"Junk, that's what. What else? And it's huge."

"It's Henry Wadsworth's trunk?"

"Yeah, and it just sits there in my garage taking up space, dirt and dust all over it. Filthy."

"So you don't have any use for it?"

"Maybe I do and maybe I don't. You want it?"

"Maybe I do and maybe I don't," Hack said.

21 The Windy City Is Not So Pretty

"How much did you settle on for Henry's trunk?" Gus asked Hack from the driver's seat of his pickup.

It was Monday morning. The two were headed south on a Chicago freeway. A dusting of snowflakes speckled the windshield.

"Four hundred," Hack said.

Gus said. "I hope it's worth it."

"I hope so too," Hack said.

"How'd Mattie take your making this trip?"

"Pretty well," Hack lied.

"Sure, Partner," Gus said. He'd known Mattie longer than Hack.

Hack didn't want to leave his wife and his baby, even for a few days. Mattie didn't want him to either, and she'd spelled it out.

When he suggested the Chicago trip, she asked, "Who's going to watch Sammy while I'm dragging my butt around at Berringer's?" Mattie didn't trust anyone with Sammy but herself, Hack and Sarai.

Hack said, "I'll only be gone during the time you're off work."

"How are you going to make that happen?"

"I've figured it out," Hack said. "Gus and I will take off Sunday afternoon right after you get home from Berringer's. From Ojibwa City, it's eight hours to Chicago. Berringer's is closed Sunday night and all-day Monday. We'll pick up the trunk on Monday and we'll make it back long before your dinner shift Tuesday."

"Three days?"

"Two and a half, really, if you do the math."

"Like the math in one of those quick-change scams? You take off and in the confusion you can't make it back in time and, then what do you know, I can't leave for work."

"No. Why would you say that? Of course not."

"I guess I trust you," she said, without much enthusiasm.

Her last sentence didn't offend Hack. He was used to it. It was one of her rituals, her way to remind them both that she did really trust him. Before Hack, she'd had a lot of bad experiences with men who lied like stereotypical musicians, and Hack was actually a musician.

She said, "Okay. And remind me, why is Gus going along on your little adventure?" Her suspicion towards Gus rational.

"I told you, I need Gus and his pickup. Henry's daughter says the trunk is big. No way to fit it into my Audi Fox. And Gus can help me load the trunk out of her garage and onto the box bed of his truck."

"Okay," Mattie said. "Two and half days. Not three."

"Of course," Hack said. "That's what I said."

The drive was pleasant and peaceful. Neither Gus nor Hack spoke much except to discuss where to stop for gas or food or how to find the motel in southeastern Wisconsin where they spent Sunday night.

Hack hadn't visited Chicago in years. He'd anticipated feelings of nostalgia, but this morning, headed south on the Dan Ryan, he felt none. Chicago was just another place where he'd done things and things had happened to him. Since Chicago, he'd done other things and other things had happened to him.

Ojibwa City, Minnesota, was the only town for which Hack had any feelings at all.

Reading Hack's thoughts as usual, Gus said, "I've always hated Chicago. I just came with you to remind myself why." Gus shifted his lower torso in his seat.

Hack had already noticed the telltale bulge in Gus's belt, under his coat and sweatshirt, just above his right butt cheek—a beneath-the-waistband holster, Gus's favorite.

Hack asked, "You carrying?"

"Of course."

'You know it's illegal to carry a gun in Illinois, don't you?"

Gus said, "Not if you have an Illinois permit."

"Do you have an Illinois permit?"

"No."

"Of course not," Hack said.

"You know what they say," Gus said. He followed up with the aphorism Hack had heard dozens of times from men and women illegally carrying firearms: "I'd rather be judged by twelve than carried by six."

"It'll take all twelve to carry you."

"Nice, partner," Gus said. "You willing to be one of them?"

Hack said nothing.

"Well?" Gus demanded.

"I'm thinking. My back isn't what it used to be."

They passed the White Sox ballpark. Hack didn't know its current name, which its corporate owners changed every ten minutes anyway. As far as he was concerned, the place was and always would be Comiskey Park. In a moment of weakness he might cave and call it "New" Comiskey.

Gus took an exit and drove into the South Side.

Hack recited directions from his phone and Gus followed them. A few minutes later they pulled up in front of a house at the address Henrietta Wadsworth had given Hack.

It was an old two-story house, painted a gleaming white not long ago, with an open front porch. At the top of the narrow driveway stood a small white garage, hardly big enough for one car.

Gus turned off the truck and got out on the driver's side. Hack opened the passenger door and slid out and stepped down onto the hard winter dirt by the curb.

A football bounced up the middle of the street and rolled to a stop at Gus's feet. About forty yards away, a bunch of black guys were playing football in the street. In their tee shirts and cutoffs, they looked heavyset and strong, the kind of guys who had littler muscles bulging out of their bigger muscles. Some wore red or blue bandannas. One shouted something.

Gus picked up the football and threw the guy a perfect forty-yard spiral.

Gus's throw reminded Hack that Gus had once gotten a football scholarship to the University of Minnesota but came back home after only a couple of months. To Gus, college football and college itself didn't fit into his business plan.

The guy at the other end of Gus's pass extended his arms and hands. He brought the ball in with soft fingertips and cradled it to his abdomen. A perfect catch.

Another bigger guy cupped his mouth in his hands and shouted something back. It sounded angry.

Gus walked around the back of his truck and joined Hack on the sidewalk. He grinned. "Still got the arm, don't I?"

Hack asked, "What'd that guy shout?"

Gus shrugged. "He said, 'Thanks'. What else would he say?"

They walked up the narrow sidewalk to the front door. Hack pressed the doorbell.

22 The Trunk

Heavy snow on the highways slowed them down, but Hack and Gus made it back with the trunk early Tuesday afternoon, in plenty of time for Mattie to leave for Berringer's.

As Gus drove his truck up the driveway, Hack saw Mattie standing at the back door, hands on her hips. The top of Sammy's head was visible over the top of his wrap. He seemed to have grown some hair in the two-and-a-half days Hack had been gone.

Sammy was facing inward towards her body, where all the good stuff was, including his mother's warmth and her breasts and her loving face.

Gone two and half days, Hack felt a thrill at the sight of them.

The trunk was in Gus's truck bed. It was heavy. Hack estimated seventy pounds. At four feet wide and nearly three feet high, it was also unwieldy. Gus and Hack climbed onto the truck bed and brushed the snow off it with mittened hands.

Gus stepped off the truck bed onto the ground. Hack shoved one end of the trunk into Gus's hands. He shoved the other end to the edge of the bed. He hopped down and grabbed the end still on the bed and tugged it off.

Together they carried the trunk through the garage and kitchen. Gus went first as they carried it down the stairs into the basement and laid it on the concrete floor.

Afterwards the four ate lunch together upstairs in the kitchen. The three older people swapped random stories while the newcomer watched and listened and studied. Gus took off for home and Mattie took off for work and Hack carried Sammy to his crib and his nap.

Hack grabbed a bottle of Chumpster out of the fridge. He sat on his living room chair and sipped it and thought about what to do next.

In person, Henrietta Wadsworth hadn't turned out to be as hostile as she'd seemed on the phone. She was just exhausted. She was in her mid-fifties and three very small but energetic kids were running all over her house.

She showed Hack and Gus the trunk in her garage. "I don't know what all is in it," she said. "I looked through it a couple of times, and it was just junk. But if you want it, you can have it."

The trunk was what Hack's dad had called a steamer trunk. It was upholstered in brown leather. Brass buckles on the front and sides clasped the rounded lid shut, backed up by two straps over the lid, also buckled tight.

On the front, its maker had embossed a foot-wide trademark for a manufacturer calling itself "Addison Luggage." Below the trademark, the maker had embossed in now-faded yellow letters, "Made in Chicago, Illinois, USA."

"Go ahead," Henrietta said. "Open it if you want."

Hack unsnapped the belts and the buckles and lifted the trunk lid. He glanced in. He picked up bunch of envelopes strewn across the top. All were addressed to "Henry Wadsworth," at the same address where Henry and Hack had conducted their sessions years ago.

Gus asked, "This is what you're after?"

Hack nodded and closed up the trunk again.

He asked Henrietta, "Everything in here is Henry's?"

She said, "Far as I can tell."

Hack handed Henrietta the envelope with a four one-hundred-dollar bills.

She opened the flap and peered in. She said, "You caught me at a bad time yesterday."

"It's okay," Hack said.

She smiled at them. "No, it's not," she said. "You got a long drive ahead of you. Please have a cup of coffee first."

Henrietta, Gus and Hack sipped coffee in her kitchen while the kids—her grandchildren, it turned out—ran around yelling and laughing. Every so often they paused in the kitchen to stand and make faces at Gus, a bearded behemoth who made scarier faces right back, which caused them to giggle and run away and two minutes later come back for more.

Hack tried to pump more information from Henrietta, but she deflected ably and told him nothing besides what he'd already heard, that Henrietta didn't think much of Henry as husband or father.

If she knew where Henry was, she wasn't saying.

Even after Hack got home to Ojibwa City, what with making himself Tuesday night dinner and caring for Sammy and shoveling the new snow and a few other chores which had piled up during his two-and-a-half-day absence, Hack didn't get a chance to explore the trunk.

Wednesday morning after breakfast, Mattie took Sammy to another "Mothers and Babies" event, this time indoors at the Ojibwa City Community Center. Hack went down to the basement to the trunk and pulled the straps off and unsnapped the buckles and lifted the lid.

Of course, no chance he'd find gold bars or bearer bonds—Henrietta would have grabbed them long ago.

Time to be scientific. Orderly. Organized. Hack took each item out of the trunk one at a time and placed it on his work bench. He did his best to stack similar items together, although precise classification was sometimes hard.

The top stack was personal papers: two copies of Henry's birth certificate; a diploma from a Chicago high school; and U.S. Army service documents, including Henry's Certificate of Honorable Discharge. According to the documents, Henry had been a corporal in the Vietnam War, which he'd never mentioned. But then Hack's own Marine dad never said much about Vietnam either. Random thought: did they know each other?

There was a Purple Heart decoration—on one side, George Washington, on the other side,

For Military Merit

Henry Wadsworth

Hack laid the hundreds of personal letters aside in several stacks. Maybe some music scholar desperate for a previously unexplored thesis topic would write a biography of Henry. Let that scholar read the letters. Hack wasn't going to read the private letters of someone he knew personally.

Another stack—or rather a disorganized pile—was made up of decades worth of bank statements, as well as hundreds of cancelled checks, bound mostly in broken rubber bands.

Hack was gentle with the old-fashioned 33⅓ vinyl LPs—lots of Bach, Ravel, Debussy, Thelonious Monk and a variety of Blue Note jazz albums, along with several salsa, including both Cuban and Puerto Rican styles, as well as drum ensembles from a variety of African peoples and cultures. There were even albums of traditional Indian, Chinese and Japanese music, along with several Gamelan records, as well as the first two John Prine LPs and several of Alison Krauss and Union Station.

In a small cardboard box marked "XMAS" were about a dozen 45 RPM records, including two of Louis Jordan singing jump tunes and two of John Philips Sousa marches.

The sight of the Sousa records called to Hack's mind the sound of Henry's voice, mentioning more than once how much he really loved *Stars and Stripes Forever.* Here it was.

Plus one 45 of the old-time movie star Jimmy Cagney singing two George M. Cohan songs: on one side, *Yankee Doodle Dandy*, on the other *Give My Regards To Broadway.*

There were dozens of books on music, including *The Classical Style*, by Charles Rosen; *To Be Or Not…To Bop*, by

Dizzy Gillespie; three bios of Claude Debussy and one of Bela Bartok, which Hack set aside on a chair to read himself later.

Lots more books too, which explained the trunk's weight—mostly mass-market paperbacks of detective stories and thrillers and spy novels.

Beneath the books were stacks of sheet music, including *Complete Chopin Etudes and Preludes*; Schnabel's two-volume edition of Beethoven *Piano Sonatas*, a book of Debussy preludes, Bach's *The Well-Tempered Clavier,* Parts 1 and 2, and a foot-deep stack of other classical piano music.

There was no pop song sheet music. Not because Henry didn't like pop tunes. "Go ahead and enjoy them," Henry had said, "but if you want to play them, play them by ear. If you can't play a simple tune from hearing it, learn how."

Hack created a separate stack for the two dozen or so esoteric music magazines with articles on twentieth century composers like Milton Babbitt and Elliott Carter.

Across the top of a newspaper clipping about composer John Cage. Henry had hand-written the word, *"Scam!"*

Beneath all this, at the bottom of the trunk, Hack found the yellow cardboard shoe box he'd been hoping for when he paid Henrietta four hundred dollars.

He placed the shoe box on his work bench and lifted its lid and set its lid aside.

A few recordings on different media lay inside.

He picked through them. The recordings presented in chronological order fifty years' evolution in music reproduction: one reel-to-reel tape, three cassette tapes, two CDs and one USB flash drive.

The reel-to-reel tape was labeled, *Master: Columbia, 4/13/75.*

The three cassettes bore no dates. Henry had labeled them only, *"Rhapsody, First Movement, Rhapsody, Second Movement,* and *Rhapsody, Third Movement."*

He'd labeled the CD with one word: *"New."*

The flash drive was unlabeled.

Hack placed everything back in the trunk but the shoe box with its recordings. That he left on his work bench.

23 The Music

Hack grabbed a Chumpster out of his mini-fridge and popped off the cap. He seated himself in front of his bench and stared at the shoe box.

He'd found what he thought he wanted.

He'd been wondering how to recreate Henry Wadsworth music, the music he'd heard that first Tuesday night when he'd been seventeen. The music he'd chased through years of study and practice. With what he might find in the shoe box, maybe he could make a start.

He'd have a better sense of how after he listened to it all.

How was one question. What about why?

Even if doable, it was going to take a lot of work. Was the work worth it?

The prospect lay heavy on him, one those duties a human being has to perform from time to time, like firing your incompetent but likable employee or junking your beat-up old favorite childhood toys or eulogizing at a funeral for someone you thought little of.

This task promised Hack nothing but misery, and voluntary misery at that, since right now he could stow the shoe box back in the trunk and chuck the entire business and no one would know.

Maybe Henry's music wasn't great, or even good. Maybe it was just crazy. Most who heard it thought so. Hack had never understood it himself, at least not the way he understood what went on in a Beatles song or an Adele song.

Was Henry even a good pianist? After that first Tuesday night decades ago in the empty Chicago club, Hack had heard only occasional snatches of Henry at the piano, during their sessions together, when Henry had been showing Hack how to play this or that scale or chord voicing or riff. Those sessions were decades in the past.

Why did Henry's music matter?

The work of a man's entire life might leave behind no more than an embittered family and a shoebox with songs no one listened to.

A lot of men left the embittered family, but only a few left the shoebox.

What if Henry Wadsworth was the musical genius of his century? Some future generation might listen entranced to Wadsworth music, finding everything he created clear and accessible and even obvious, the way Haydn's music sometimes seemed obvious, now that every composer who came after him had learned from it—even the ones who themselves had never heard of Haydn. Future generations might develop a new musical language rooted in Henry's music.

Music was always changing. Time and history might bring into the world an audience smart and deep and equipped to appreciate Henry. They'd wonder why Henry's own contemporaries had been deaf to his genius.

It was possible. Taste in music changes fast, not just from century to century, but from year to year. As a twelve-year-old, Hack had considered the rock songs favored by seventeen-year-olds dated and stupid.

Didn't Henry deserve to be recognized for being so far ahead of his time?

What good is recognition to a dead man?

Unanswerable question.

Without any help from anyone, Hack could play the CD and get whatever music was there off the flash drive, but he'd need help with the tapes.

He called Gus and asked, "Do you know where I can get either a reel-to-reel tape player or a cassette player?"

Gus said, "I don't know about a reel-to-reel, but I've got a cassette deck."

"Really? Why?"

"What do you mean, why? To listen to music."

"Isn't a cassette deck obsolete? Like some kind of seventies thing?"

"Sure," Gus said. "This one was my dad's."

"And you still use it?"

"Why change what works?"

Hack said, "Since I need one, I suppose I can't complain."

"Let me guess," Gus said. "There's something you found in Henry's trunk you want to listen to?"

"Good guess."

"Bring it on over."

"I have three cassette tapes of his," Hack said. "Can we copy them while I'm there?"

"Sure," Gus said. "I always keep a supply of blank cassettes around here."

"Why?"

"I like to record albums off the FM radio."

"You're joking, right?"

"Maybe I am and maybe I'm not."

Hack put his three precious Henry cassettes in a laptop case and put on his boots and coat and drove to Gus's house.

The driving was easy. Plows had cleared the roads after the snowfall, which piled up only six to eight inches anyway. Hack drove County 15 past a few miles of barren winter farmland and then through the beginnings of the jack pine forest. He turned right and drove up the long gravel road to Gus's place, which was located on the edge of the true thicker forest.

As Hack pulled up, Gus came out of his white farmhouse. It was nippy, but Gus wore no coat, just jeans and an old Vikings sweatshirt, probably sized a whole bunch of X's followed by an L.

Hack opened the driver door and got out.

First thing, Gus asked, "When did you have your last oil change?"

Hack said, "I don't know."

"You wouldn't," Gus said. He checked the windshield sticker and then the odometer and shook his head. He took personal offense at what he considered Hack's neglect for the basic maintenance on the machine he'd hand-rebuilt.

"Pull into the shed," Gus said. Gus did his auto work in his 14-foot by 14-foot green shed.

Hack did as told. He got out of his car and leaned against the wall and watched. Gus drained the oil and replaced the filter. Gus poured in the new oil and topped off the transmission and washer fluids.

"You haven't wrecked it," Gus conceded.

"It runs," Hack said.

They left the Audi in the shed and walked over to Gus's white frame house and into it.

Inside, Hack found Gus's son LG lounging on the living room couch, reading a used paperback of *The Federalist Papers*.

"Uncle Hack," LG said. He unfolded himself and stood and gave Hack a hug and a complicated fist-bumping greeting Hack did his best to keep up with.

Hack said, "If you go back to calling me 'Uncle Hack', I'm going to have to go back to calling you 'Little Gus'."

LG was a younger leaner version of his father, "little" only by comparison.

"Sorry. I forgot for a minute," LG said. "Dad says you've got some music you want to listen to."

"I do," Hack said.

Then to Gus, "I can't get over the fact you still use a cassette deck."

"Then why'd you call and ask me if I have one?" Gus asked.

Hack said, "I hoped you might have one in that attic of yours, where you keep everything the Dropo family owned since its claim-jumping days."

"I think they started brewing Chumpsters about the same time," Gus pointed out. "You still drink them." He went into the kitchen.

LG said, "Dad sticks with what works."

"Doesn't he have a CD player?" Hack asked.

LG said, "Nope."

"No Internet streaming service?"

"That's my department," LG said. "It's nothing but cassette tapes for my dad. And you should hear what's on them."

"Like?"

"Like Starland Vocal Band? Leo Sayer? Loggins and Messina? Grandpa music. My actual grandpa's music, actually. Dad inherited them when grandpa died. I don't think my dad has bought a single new tape of his own his whole life."

"Gus has never been a spender," Hack said. "Why are you home, anyway?"

"I'm on break from school."

"What year are you in college, anyway?" Hack asked. "Like a sophomore or junior?"

"I'm in graduate school," LG said. "Going for my PhD in Mechatronics Engineering."

"I won't ask what that is," Hack said.

Gus came back with two cold Chumpster bottles in his left hand and one for himself in his right. He passed the two from his left hand to LG and Hack in order.

LG lay back on the couch, beer propped on his stomach. Hack sat with his on the rug nearby. Gus inserted the cassette into his deck and took a seat on his big papa chair.

They listened to Henry's first cassette, labeled *Rhapsody. First Movement.*

The sound quality was awful. Henry's tinny-sounding piano was barely audible through the noise of chattering people and clinking glasses and clattering plates. Entire passages disappeared in the din.

Playing the entire cassette took about fifteen minutes, only about five of which contained audible piano playing.

"At least there were some people there to hear him," Hack commented.

"That's the guy who inspired you to study music all those years?" Gus asked Hack.

"This tape is not a fair representation," Hack said. "You can't even hear him."

Gus said, "And hearing him is what did it?"

"Absolutely," Hack said. "Is there a way to convert my cassette tapes to a computer file? Maybe I can clean up the music on my computer."

LG said, "I've got a device for that. Once in a while there's a song of grandpa's I like."

"Could you use it to copy all three of my cassettes?"

"Sure," LG said. He got up and removed the cassette from the deck. Hack handed him the other two cassettes from out of his laptop bag.

"It won't take long," LG said. He went into his bedroom.

"Don't say anything," Hack told Gus.

"I remember when four hundred dollars was a lot of money, Partner."

"You're saying something."

"Yeah, I am," Gus admitted. "What are you planning to do with these tapes?"

"I'm going to perform the music in a concert," Hack said to his own surprise. He must have made the decision without noticing.

"Why?"

"It needs to be out there."

"Again, why?"

"Never mind."

"Does that mean you don't know? Or that or you do know but you don't want to say?"

"Both."

"Thanks for clearing that up," Gus said.

LG came back into the room. He handed Hack the three cassettes and a flash drive.

"It's all on the flash drive," he said. "I'm curious to see what you can do with it."

"So am I," Hack said.

24 The Music Librarian

LG's flash drive with the music from the three cassettes
was a bust. On all three, the piano was too far away from
the mike and the crowd noise was too loud.

Maybe in L.A. or Nashville there was a multi-million-dollar
music studio where some genius engineer could extract
music from it, but Hack didn't have that studio and he
wasn't that engineer.

On first listen, Henry's CD—the one Henry had labeled
"New"—was also a bust.

The CD was obviously home recorded, and badly. It
contained only about twenty minutes of music, most of
which consisted of little snatches of barely audible piano,
repeating only the same few tunes, varied sometimes by
rhythm and chord.

There were also a few bits of Henry humming in his
familiar off-key baritone, which made Hack smile. Henry
never could sing.

These snatches of melody could have been a way of
recording ideas for some composition Henry wrote. They
were useless to Hack.

Hack laid the CD aside and did some calling around. It
turned out the Music Library at Ojibwa College of Minnesota
had a reel-to-reel tape machine.

Hack drove the mile across town to the College with his
laptop case on the passenger seat. He couldn't zip the top of
the case over the reel-to-reel tape. Its rim popped out the
open top. It was too big around.

The Department of Music Studies had its own shiny new
building. The library inside was a brightly lit space with hard
floors, high ceilings, rows of bookcases and a dozen mostly
unoccupied computer stations spread here and there.

The librarian was easy to spot. He was sitting in an
enclosed area in the back behind a low desk with a computer
on it, keying in information about some new-looking DVDs

stacked in front of him on the counter. He saw Hack approach and stopped typing. He said, "May I help you?"

"Yes. I'm Hack Wilder. We spoke on the phone."

"Oh yes, the reel-to-reel request." He smiled. "We don't get many of those."

He was a thin man, balding in front, his remaining brown hair hanging straight down to his shoulders. He looked about forty. Over the phone, he'd told Hack his name was Graham Hamner.

Hamner said, "May I see the tape, Mr. Wilder?"

Hack took the tape out of his laptop case and laid in on the counter.

"My, that's a nice-looking tape." Which was true.

Hack said, "I think it might be professional."

Hamner asked, "What would you like to do with it?"

"I'd like to hear it. Then, it there's anything worthwhile on it, I'd like to copy it to a computer file. I brought an empty flash drive with me. Do you have the equipment for that?"

"Yes, we can do that. What's on the tape?"

"I'm not sure," Hack said. "The label is suggestive."

Hamner picked up the tape and read the label aloud. *"Master: Columbia, 4/13/75."* He asked, "Is this some sort of music performance for a record label?"

"I hope so."

"Of whom?"

"I hope it's a recording of Henry Wadsworth."

"Henry Wadsworth? I don't recognize that name," Hamner said. "And I thought I knew the name of most recorded musicians. It's part of my job."

"I don't know if this is a commercial recording," Hack said. "I don't know where it came from, actually. I don't even know for sure it's Henry. That's why I want to hear it."

Hamner swiveled in his chair to face his computer monitor. While Hack stood and waited, Hamner typed. After a few minutes, he said, "There's no Henry Wadsworth listed in any of the catalogs. He was almost certainly never commercially recorded."

"And yet I have this tape," Hack said. "It seems commercial quality. Like a master recording."

"True. And it's a chance to broaden my knowledge." Hamner smiled in evident pleasure. He leaned forward and said, as if he were passing on a secret, "I don't get the chance to do that every day around here."

"I suppose not," Hack said in sincere sympathy.

"Well, please step back into my lair with me and let's just see."

Hamner led Hack to the back of his librarian enclosure. He unlocked the door of an eight-by-twelve room. Hack followed him in. A two-foot-high reel-to-reel tape machine sat upright on a table.

The machine had two mounts for tapes. The right hand one held an empty tape reel. The left mount was empty. Hamner mounted Hack's reel on the left side mount and threaded the tape from it through the mechanism to the empty reel on the right.

Hamner hit a few buttons.

A solo pianist began to play the Duke Ellington tune, *Take The A Train*.

"Nice," Hamner said. "Is that your man?"

"I think it's Henry," Hack said. After another thirty seconds, "I'm sure of it."

Hack's reel contained nine takes and no retakes, in high fidelity stereo. It sounded like the final product of a professional recording session, mixed, mastered, and ready to release into the market.

The nine tracks were all covers. Henry played two tunes by Duke Ellington—*C Jam Blues* and *Do Nothing Till You Hear From Me*; two by the Gershwins—*Lady Be Good* and *Summertime*; two Thelonious Monk tunes—*Bemsha Swing* and *Ask Me Now*; the Beatles song, *Things We Said Today*; and a simultaneously haunting but swinging performance of the Hank Williams country classic, *I'm So Lonesome I Could Cry*. There was even a Bach fugue for keyboard.

The tape contained nothing Henry had composed himself.

Hamner said, "What an excellent pianist. Extraordinary, really. But he's turning simple tunes into really complex explorations. His music would demand a lot from the listener. I wonder if that's why they never released this recording."

"There could be a lot of reasons," Hack said, thinking of all Henry's ups and downs. "Many, many reasons."

"Maybe it was the Bach fugue," Hamner said. "Maybe the record company didn't want that on a nonclassical record."

"Maybe," Hack said. "Or maybe Henry himself refused to release it."

"Why would he do that?"

"It's not his music."

25 Flashback

The next morning Hack sat on his work bench chair and mounted the flash drive in his basement laptop.

His screen displayed a couple of dozen icons on the drive. Most were icons for sound files.

Each icon had name, for example, *Rhapsody 27*, or *In A Nasty Mood*, or *Grafito*, with the word "version" and a number.

He clicked on the icon called *Rhapsody 27, Version 1*. His computer's music player app kicked in. A feeble string orchestra sounded in the laptop's tinny speaker.

Hack clicked again to stop the player.

Hack spent the next few minutes cabling his big basement speakers into a device through which he could connect them to his laptop.

He clicked on *Rhapsody 27* again. This time the music signal passed from his computer through the device and through his speakers.

Music thundered through his basement. It started with a string orchestra. Henry joined the orchestra at the piano, followed by horns and woodwinds, finally by African percussion.

As the music drove ahead, Henry's piano changed roles from moment to moment. Sometimes his piano took the melodic lead in front of the orchestra, sometimes it switched to a call-and-response pattern and took turns with the orchestra, sometimes the orchestra went silent and the piano drove ahead, heedless whether the orchestra was there at all.

It was a fierce music, always fast, but fastest when most quiet, always dense in its harmonies and complex in its rhythms.

Rhapsody 27 was nothing but Henry's piano playing writ large. It was the style of music Hack had heard in that Chicago bar when he was seventeen, only now with an orchestra.

The piece lasted twenty-two minutes before it ended, not with a bang, but more like a Debussy whimper.

Of course, *The Sunken Cathedral.*

Very early it became obvious the orchestra wasn't genuine. Engineers and computer programmers had worked to develop their ability to copy the sounds of genuine acoustic instruments.

Progress had been real but limited; it was still possible to distinguish the sounds of genuine acoustic instruments from their synthesized copies, and Henry's strings, horns, woodwinds, and percussion were all synthesized.

With one exception. Hack couldn't tell if the piano was synthesized too. It sounded not only like a genuine acoustic piano, but like a great acoustic piano.

But where would Henry get access to a piano that good? And how would he have recorded it?

If it was a synthesized piano, where could Hack get one for himself? The real thing costs tens of thousands of dollars.

Logic dictated the piano must be synthesized too.

To create this recording, Henry must have taught himself how to use a music sequencing computer program—software which allowed the musician to record and edit complicated pieces of music with many instrumental voices.

A lot of musicians did this kind of thing, although not on Henry's scale or at his degree of difficulty. Often a lounge singer or guitar-toting folk singer set up with pre-recorded drum machine and bass. Early in his career, before Benedetto graduated to genuine symphony orchestras, he'd made lush pre-recorded violin backgrounds part of his busking.

Hack had done a little sequencing himself, but for simple tunes using only a few voices.

When Henry had created and recorded this own fake orchestra, he'd upped the degree of difficulty past anything Hack had heard before.

To record a complete simulated symphony orchestra, Henry would have had first to compose all the instrumental parts, then, one at a time, perform on a keyboard and record his own execution of each synthesized instrument's part.

The recording of *Rhapsody 27* sounded like a full symphony orchestra. An orchestra can contain one hundred musicians, perhaps 16 First Violins, 16 Second Violins, 12 Violas, 12 Cellos, 8 Double Basses, 4 Flutes, 4 Oboes, 4 Clarinets, 4 Bassoons, English Horns, 4 trumpets, 4 trombones, 1 tuba, and others.

Henry's *Rhapsody* 27 also incorporated hand percussion and an American-style trap drum kit.

The ultimate musical isolation—one human being posing as more than a hundred.

Hack wondered if the sheet music was on the flash drive. Hack took another look. Six of the files were PDFs, a format for document files.

One of the PDFs was labeled *Rhapsody 27*. Hack opened it.

It was the sheet music for the recording he'd just heard, the entire orchestral score for the piece, including written parts for strings, horns and woodwinds, even drum notation for a trap set.

Hack looked for a written piano part. There was none.

It turned out Henry had recorded *Rhapsody 27* with piano in versions 1 through 5. Hack spent the next two hours listening to all of them. In five versions, everything was identical but the piano part. Henry played a different piano part each time.

Henry had entitled the sixth *Revolution 27* recording with the additional word *Karaoke*.

The *Rhapsody 27 Karaoke* version was note-for-note identical to the others, except that there was no piano at all, just empty places for a pianist to fill by playing something

It turned out that all the three dozen of sound files on the flash drive amounted to only six different compositions, each identical except for the varying piano parts, and each with one *Karaoke* version which included no piano at all.

Six compositions.

If there was no written music for the piano, how did Henry know what to play?

A story held it that a witness had seen Mozart conduct and perform a famous piano concerto along with an orchestra without any written piano music for himself. Since the concerto is nowadays played all over the world, Mozart must have written down a piano part sometime.

In 1923, Paul Whiteman had held the world premiere of *Rhapsody In Blue* before George Gershwin had the chance to write down his complete piano part. At the first performance, when Gershwin finished a solo piano passage, there was nothing written to tell the conductor Whiteman that it was time for the orchestra to resume playing. Gershwin hand signaled him.

Mozart and Gershwin might have already known what they were going to play. Or they might have improvised. Or both.

Henry Wadsworth had played a completely different piano part—often wildly different—on every recording of these six otherwise identical pieces.

Was that intentional?

Knowing Henry, probably. Most jazz composers design their music anticipating some amount of improvisation.

And Henry could deliver.

Another question: had Henry ever had the chance to perform any of this music live with a real symphony?

Had Henry gotten any chance at all to perform live, perhaps at a club, along with his pre-recorded orchestra, the way Benedetto did with his recordings?

Hack had seen no evidence of it.

Hack wrote emails to Botman and Hatfield asking the same questions and got back negative answers. Botman hadn't heard of or seen any evidence of Henry performing live in decades. And it was Botman's job to know. Hatfield had nothing either.

If Hack tried to play piano on this *Rhapsody*, for instance, using Henry's pre-recorded *Karaoke* version as background, what would Hack play?

He could listen to what Henry played on the five versions and copy one of them. Hack would face a lot of work to memorize anyone of these, not to mention the inevitable technical challenges of trying to match Henry's virtuosity.

Time to get to work.

26 A Concert

Months passed.

Sammy grew and developed just the way his mother and father hoped. He got a full head of hair. His babbles started to sound like English. He crawled. They baby-proofed the house. He got pretty quick and agile and tried to outsmart them, but they kept him safe anyway.

One spring Sunday afternoon just before 4 PM, Hack sat behind his electric keyboard on his portable stool in Max's Madhouse.

Gus had suggested the Madhouse wasn't the perfect venue for a concert of Henry's music. "Maybe take it somewhere they like that kind of stuff."

To which Hack responded, "Every Saturday night I go to the Madhouse and play music everybody likes. Why can't I just this once go there and play something else, even if I'm the only one who likes it?"

Gus asked him, "You're talking about playing this Wadsworth opus of yours on a Madhouse Saturday night?"

"Sunday afternoon will do fine. Might as well not blow our only gig."

At Mattie's insistence, a grumbling Max agreed to close the restaurant area for two hours just this once, on this one single Sunday afternoon.

For the next two hours—and not one minute longer—the Madhouse would somehow get along without trays clanking or glasses clinking or dishes clattering.

Because Hack brought more equipment than usual, he needed more space than available on the little stage from which he usually played.

Gus and he had laid down some risers at the front of the big restaurant space. To the left of Hack and his keyboard sat

212

a customer table for four he and Gus had carried onto the risers from the restaurant section. On the table, Hack had configured his laptop, his networking devices and his sound mixing equipment.

He and Gus had spread four speakers around the room and two monitor speakers in front of the keyboard for Hack himself. They'd wired the laptop directly into the mixing equipment, which in turn fed the speakers.

With ten minutes to go, Hack recognized everyone who'd come.

No surprise there. Promo was minimal. Mattie had sent out some emails and made some phone calls. Max had posted the announcement on the *Special Events* page of the Madhouse website:

One Time Only!
Henry Wadsworth Music
This Sunday at 4 PM!

Indoors was snug and warm. Heavy snow was falling outside. The snow would deter curiosity seekers. But Ojibwa City people were used to winter and they'd make it if they wanted to.

Sylvia sat in the leftmost chair of the front row. Mattie sat to Sylvia's right, with Sammy hanging in his sling in front of her, facing out, head leaning down, eyes closed in sleep. Mattie was determined to keep lugging him in her sling even as he grew bigger and heavier. She might have been strong enough to carry it off a little longer.

Mrs. Malkin and Mrs. Paige also sat in the front row, on the far right. They'd dressed as if for a Symphony Concert, in dark suits and small tasteful hats. They held their black clutch purses on their laps in front of them. Mrs. Malkin smiled at Hack.

Hack's ex-wife Lily Lapidos was sitting with their daughter Sarai in the middle of an otherwise empty middle row. They gave Hack palms-up half-moon-shaped waves of moral support.

Former Ojibwa City Mayor Buster Skoglund had helped Hack and Gus set up the 48 chairs. Now he slouched on one of them in the back row, dozing. His trip had been quick; he lived in the Madhouse and spent winters sleeping just inside the back door.

Gus's husky Shakey Dropo had dropped by as well. He was asleep in the far corner, tail covering his nose, his round white belly twitching as he chased elusive Arctic hares in his dreams.

So far, even counting Shakey, Hack's audience numbered fewer than a dozen.

Rolf Johnson and his wife Debra walked in and took seats in the back row, several seats from Buster. They both wore full Deputy Sheriff regalia, khaki uniforms, wide black Sam Browne belts, guns, sticks and mace. Must be planning to go on duty later.

Gus was fiddling with the mixing equipment at the table next to Hack. He'd helped with the sound check and was going to monitor the sound quality in the room while Hack played.

Neither of Hack's other bandmates Mel or Baz had shown up yet, although they'd promised to.

LG walked in with three young friends, including a stocky guy about LG's age, an athletic blonde woman with bared midriff, and a thin tattooed redhead girl pierced in every facial feature pierceable, including bejeweled septum nose ring, nose studs in each nostril, a tiny gold upper lip ring, one silvery ring in her right eyebrow, and two hoop earrings. She positively twinkled.

Hack saw no one he recognized from Ojibwa College except the Music Librarian Graham Hamner, who sat alone front row middle, eyes gleaming in anticipation.

Laghdaf walked in with the same serene Muslim woman Hack had met at Sam and Aviva's wedding. Her name was Maryam.

Following Laghdaf and Maryam, Sam Lapidos strolled in with his new wife Aviva.

Lily and Sarai got up from their chairs. There was a lot of handshaking and hugging and kissing. They all sat together in a sixsome in the middle of the otherwise empty row.

Hack knew every audience member personally. No strangers. This was good, right?

Hack glanced down and saw the true strangers, all 88 of them, arrayed in a wide row of white keys which dazzled even in the dim Madhouse ceiling lights. Among each seven white keys were interspersed five black keys in a repeating pattern of twos and threes.

Soon he'd have to start using these keys to make sounds. Now wasn't the time to ask what sounds. He tried never to practice or even to think about any music the same day he was going to perform it. Ms. Lager said that could take the edge off. Maybe this was just another superstition, like his superstition against studying the same day as a math test.

This system hadn't worked for math.

Hack had never understood why those pro boxers worked up such a sweat before a bout. Why wear yourself out just to wear yourself out again? Shouldn't you save your strength? Shouldn't you relax?

Relax—there's the nub. He shrugged his shoulders up and down and craned his neck and swung his arms around. He inhaled and exhaled several deep breaths in a row.

He'd start playing when someone or something kicked the music off, the computer or himself—Hack didn't remember which. Hack's hands would take over, driven by the knowledge they'd acquired over years of grueling practice in his monomaniacal youth, or perhaps better informed by the study he'd put in for the past months, getting ready for this one-time performance.

The main thing was to relax.

But then again, the knowledge was in his mind, not his hands. His mind drove his hands and fingers.

Relax. If he relaxed, the music could come through from his mind the way he'd heard it come through Henry's.

If Hack clenched in his body or in his attention or in his mind, he'd choke off the music, and it would stay stuck inside him where no one else could hear it.

Relax.

Gus stood in front of Hack and said a brief something to the crowd. Must be an introduction. Must be 4 PM. Polite applause. The Madhouse ceiling lights dimmed even more than usual. Who did that? Buster?

Hack's mind was as empty as Max's kitchen and Max's bar and most of Max's chairs.

Henry's synthesized drums sounded the beginning of the *Karaoke* version of *Grafito*, one of the three pieces Hack had picked to play.

Hack started with the *Karaoke* version of *Grafito* because *Grafito* was the easiest of the three.

Which wasn't saying much. The first three minutes passed with no melody, only African rhythms in an ever-more complicated polyrhythm, soon joined by random-sounding snatches of odd dissonant chords from the synthetic brass. On cue, Hack came in on keyboard, playing note for note what Henry had played in his fourth and final recording of the piece, just as Hack had memorized it.

Grafito ended with an explosion of sound from Henry's entire prerecorded ensemble, including orchestra and drums. Hack thundered out fistfuls of notes in rolling piano chords.

Polite applause from the people in their chairs.

Hack waited out his pre-recorded one-minute pause, head down, eyes on the keyboard.

Hack began the second piece, the *Karaoke* of the piece Henry called *Procrastination,* which was a perfect name. It was a "rhythm changes" tune, taking its chords from the old song *I Got Rhythm.*

It began with Hack dithering along solo on his keyboard, making a series of melodic false starts which never amounted to anything, feints towards resolutions which never came, stories begun but never quite told. It was like time-lapse photography, ocean waves pounding on the shore, slow and uncertain, pointless beyond their own insistence.

Music has the power to move human emotion. Music can excite or thrill or sadden. Music can drive away the blues or bring them on. Music can inspire any feeling or combination of feelings.

It's a rare composer who can create music with a sense of humor, and Henry had done it.

It had taken Hack half a dozen listens before he got the joke.

As Hack dawdled through *Procrastination,* he realized he was hitting some wrong notes, wrong because they were different from the ones Henry had played.

He realized he'd turned the beat around—what had once been the fourth beat was now the second beat of the measure. Should he fix it?

Henry's recorded ensemble had kicked in, crafted from high trumpets and flutes, with a rumbling bass adding tension at the bottom.

The music should have been a train wreck, but it wasn't. *Procrastination* was surviving Hack's fumble-fingered goofs with no apparent loss.

The hell with it. If Hack understood Henry's plan, and he was sure he did, he could play his own version of Henry's idea, and *Procrastination* would survive whole and healthy.

That's what Hack did. As far as Hack was concerned, *Procrastination* stayed funny all the way through, and fun to play as well.

Hack finished *Procrastination* to a slightly more enthusiastic smattering of mild applause. A few chuckles came from the direction of Sam Lapidos.

Hack waited out the second pre-programmed pause with his hands relaxed on his lap and his eyes closed.

Henry's synthesized string orchestra sounded the beginnings of *Rhapsody 27 Karaoke* through the speakers.

Hack's cue came and he joined the music on his keyboard, playing his piano part, or rather Henry's, exactly as Henry had played it on the first recording of the *Rhapsody.*

Hack knew Henry's melody lines, the chords and their voicings, the rhythms, the riffs, the explosions and the whispers, all of it, and he knew he could play them all, for twenty-two minutes from beginning to end.

But why? Why add nothing new? Was that what Henry wanted? For his student Hack Wilder to do a perfect impression of Henry Wadsworth?

"Play what you hear, not what you know."

Hack heard not only Henry's choices, but the ideas behind them, and from those ideas he began to make choices himself.

A new thing happened which had not happened before. As Hack immersed in the new music he was inventing in collaboration with Henry, he perceived not only the music but the room and himself in the front of the room and the others in the room with him.

He was no longer a monk in a cell in the Beehive. Not trapped in the hard effort of extracting the right music from inside him, Hack became more aware than he had ever been of the world around him and the people in it.

Is one of the ceiling lights flickering?

Has Max's floor always been that gashed and notched and scored with cigarette burns?

A stranger comes into the Madhouse, late for the show—a muscular young man with a buzzcut on the side and big brush on the top, wearing a black leather coat down to his knees. The stranger finds an empty chair and slips into it

Buster Skoglund gets up and leaves—bathroom break so soon?

Mrs. Malkin is still sitting there, frowning, her face tightened by an intent expression, but Mrs. Paige's chair is empty.

From Mattie's lap, Sammy is watching his dad. Sammy is wearing the same expression he wore the first time he solved that stacking cups puzzle, serious and intent.

The idea comes. Why not?

It's Hack's solo. He can play anything he wants, anything he hears, and what he hears right now is a voice. It's Henry humming the old Sousa march, *Stars and Stripes Forever.*

Hack beats out the march rhythm and chords with his left hand and the tune with his right.

A ceiling light in the back is blinking almost in rhythm—or is it just that the bulb's burning out?

Sammy starts waving his arms around. From behind him, Mattie gently grabs his hands and begins to clap them together in time with the music. When she lets go, he keeps on clapping in time, the brilliance of his delighted smile lighting the world.

Henry's orchestra comes back in.

Hack is relaxed, more relaxed than he's been, maybe in his life. That's why his hands and fingers fly over the keys, playing what he hears, only it's himself making the music he's hearing, and at the same time he sees the entire room, as if immersing himself in the music has in its remarkable and perverse way intensified his awareness of everything not the music.

Henry had created his disciplined and organized sound for the sake of freedom. Within this wide world of possibility Henry had created, Hack was free.

26 The Reviews Come In

After the concert, Hack's usual crew jammed two tables together instead of the usual single table for six.

Of course, the usual six were there: Mattie, Gus, Sylvia, Rolf, Debra, and sometimes Sarai. Just as the letter "y" sometimes counts as a vowel along with a, e, i, o, and u," so Sarai sometimes sat with the grownups, although she'd not yet managed to snag herself so much as a single sip of beer.

They needed the extra table because of the others who'd made the drive from the Twin Cities and now stuck around,like Hack's ex-wife Lily, who of course was also Sarai's mother, as well as Laghdaf and his companion Maryam.

It turned out the man who came in during Hack's piano solo was Hatfield McGray himself. Hack waved him over and introduced him to everyone. He took a chair at the end of the second table.

Lily grabbed her chance to hold Sammy and he sat on Lily's lap facing the other humans. He continued to say little. Sometimes he turned to reach up and feel this unfamiliar woman's face. Lily let him poke her cheeks and nose and chin, but with practiced ease deflected and redirected his hands and fingers any time they came near her eyes.

Sam and Aviva couldn't stay. Sam was in the middle of his federal trial. While he waited outside with his car running, Aviva came by the table and said to Hack, "Performing in public always terrifies me. You seem very self-assured up there."

"Mostly," Hack said, "But there were a few moments when I almost got discombobulated."

Aviva patted his hand and goodbyed everyone and left.

"I'm not so sure about what you said there, Partner," Gus told Hack. "You seemed completely combobulated the whole time."

Hack asked with suspicion, "What's wrong with that?

"Nothing," Gus said, "In fact it's good. Very good. If being discombobulated is bad, being combobulated must be good."

Sylvia said to Gus, "You don't know what that means, do you?"

Gus asked, "What?"

"Either one," she replied. "Discombobulated or combobulated."

"I do too," he said.

"Then tell us," Sylvia demanded.

Lily leaned forward to watch the dialog with open curiosity. From her lap, Sammy looked the direction Lily was looking.

"I don't think I will," Gus said to Sylvia.

"Why not?"

"Why should I?"

"To show me you can."

"Sure I can."

"Then why won't you show me?"

"Because you're trying to make me show you, that's why. I don't do things people try to make me do."

Lily asked Mattie, "Is this normal?"

Mattie answered, "We think it might be some kind of foreplay."

Hack wondered if the entire afternoon was going to go like this, everyone talking about everything but the music. trying to distract him, or worse, to be extra-nice—a bad sign. Why didn't they just come straight out with it?

Right after Hack's concert ended, Laghdaf had said to Hack, "I hope you're not disappointed by the turnout. And as is said, Wadsworth music will never be popular."

"I'm not disappointed," Hack said. And he wasn't. But it would be nice if somebody said something.

LG and his three friends came over from the bar, which Max had reopened even while the final chord was still sounding through the Madhouse. LG gave his dad a fist bump. Gus returned the bump with his left hand and saluted back with the Chumpster bottle in his right.

LG said to Hack, "We're on our way out, but we wanted to say thanks."

LG was young. He might be candid. Hack asked him, "What did you think of the music?"

"Honestly?"

Hack said, "Yes, please. Honestly."

LG opened his mouth and closed it again.

"I said, honestly."

LG shrugged. "It was okay. You know, not my taste." He turned to his three friends. "What did you guys think?"

His stocky male friend imitated LG's shrug. "Okay, I guess."

The athletic blonde said, "It was very confusing. I admit I couldn't quite follow all of it. Some parts were nice, though. I liked the quiet parts. And I really liked the part when you played that old march—I don't know its name."

Which left only Pierced Girl, still sparkling from various parts of her head, who said, "I loved the whole thing. Every note. It was all beautiful."

LG asked her, "You didn't find it weird or hard to follow?"

She shook her head. "Not at all. Clear as could be. And romantic and beautiful, like one of those hundred-year-old songs, only longer and richer, like a symphony, and full of—"

she paused—"mystery and depth." She smiled a twinkling smile at Hack. "Thank you."

"You're welcome," Hack said, "Maybe I didn't do Henry's music justice. It would have been better if Henry had played it himself."

"No," Pierced Girl said, "It was better this way."

"Really?" Hack asked, "Why?"

"If this Henry guy who wrote it was the only one who could play it, it wouldn't be a real composition, would it? A composition has to be something other people can play too and keep alive that way."

"That's an interesting thing to say," Hack said. "Do you play music yourself?"

"No, I'm just a fan. I'm studying nuclear engineering," she said. "Why?"

"Just curious," Hack said. "Thanks."

"It's all true," she said. "Bye." She turned to leave. LG gave a small wave and followed her. The other two did too, leaving behind the twelve at the double table: Hack and Mattie; Gus and Sylvia; Rolf and Debra; Laghdaf and Maryam; Hatfield, Lily and Sarai, as well as Sammy, who watched the older humans with his usual intense curiosity, as if their antics would make sense if he just tried harder.

Shakey walked over, maybe hoping for beer, which Gus was known to give him from time to time, despite Sylvia's vehement disapproval.

Shakey took a place by Lily, staring up at Sammy with adoration. He tried to lick Sammy's foot, but Lily shifted Sammy out of reach with a deft maneuver. Shakey settled across her feet to wait for his next chance. She let him.

Gus told Hack, "Well, you got your man Henry at least one new fan."

Hack said, "I guess."

"Which makes your concert a success," Maryam said, one of the few times Hack had ever heard her speak.

Laghdaf smiled at Maryam and said, "I promised you that we'd hear something different today."

"And you kept your promise," she said.

Rolf's wife Debra said to Hack, "What you said about Henry a minute ago, that got me thinking. I mean, what if you could bring Henry back to play his own music?"

"How would he do that?" Rolf asked his wife. "This isn't one of your time travel theories again, is it?"

"No," she said with exaggerated patience. "This is not one of my time travel theories. But if it was, it would be a wonderful thing, wouldn't it? To hear Henry Wadsworth play his own music?"

Rolf asked her, "Do you even like that music?"

Debra kept mum.

Sylvia asked her, "You believe in time travel?'

"Physicists haven't ruled it out," Debra said.

Sylvia said, "But aren't there are paradoxes that make time travel impossible? If we went back to bring Henry Wadsworth to here and now, that would change the past. Maybe if he went back, he wouldn't have written any music, or at least the same music."

"That may not be a problem," Sarai piped in.

"What do you mean?" Sylvia asked her.

"We were studying about that in our science class," Sarai said. "Maybe it's like Einstein wrote."

Hack asked his daughter, "What did Einstein write?"

Sarai answered, "This old friend of his had died. Another old scientist he worked with. He was trying to make the widow feel better. He wrote her a letter."

Sarai took her phone out of her pocket. Everybody waited to hear what Einstein had written. Sarai was swift on her phone. Her fingers and thumbs flew over it as close to light speed as Einstein allowed.

After only a few seconds, Sarai said, "Here it is. He wrote the widow a letter. He wrote, "People like us, who believe in physics, know that the distinction between past, present and future is only a stubbornly persistent illusion."

Her dad said, "So?"

"So," she answered, "What if Einstein was right? Maybe before and after are only illusions, and there's this sort of fabric of space-time, and even if we could travel in time we can't change the past?"

"What if, indeed," Hack said to his daughter.

"It's like time and space are this elastic thing, and no matter how we stretch the elastic, afterwards it snaps back into its original shape. So nothing in the fabric can be changed."

"Nothing?" Sylvia asked.

Sarai said, "Well, maybe there might be a few stretch marks."

"Stretch marks?" Mattie said. "Tell me about it."

"What do you mean?" Sarai asked,

"Never mind," her mother Lily told her. "With luck, you'll find out for yourself."

"Who are you kidding?" Sylvia said to Mattie. "You haven't stretched in the slightest."

Sylvia's point was a good one. As far as Hack could tell—and he'd examined with meticulous attention—Mattie had snapped back to her original shape almost immediately after giving birth. All that pregnancy yoga must have paid off.

It was obvious everyone was determined to talk about anything and everything but the music they'd heard. So what? Their job was to be his friends, not music critics. Anyway, he despised critics, and he needed all the friends he could get.

Mattie sat closest to him, almost leaning against him, her left hand resting light on Hack's right forearm. Her warmth was a salve to every wound he could ever experience. She sat protective as a she-wolf, ready to leap at anyone who said a negative word. But no one here would do that.

Hack had accomplished what he wanted. Henry's music was on the brink of extinction, but Hack had staved off the extinction for now.

As well as the memory of Henry Wadsworth the man?

Hack couldn't revive a detailed memory of Henry; in fact, most of Hack's own past was a blur. Hack had forgotten almost all of the thousands of gigs he'd played since Henry first suggested the possibility, and most of the things Henry told him, and most of the adventures he'd had with Gus.

And that squabble with Mattie a few days ago? What had that one been about?

So what? Play what you hear, not what you know. A permanent invitation to the present.

Hatfield McGray spoke. "This is all a lot of fun, and I'm learning some things"—he nodded at Sarai—"but I came here for a reason."

"What's that?" Hack asked him.

"I wanted to tell you something," Hatfield said.

"Something about the music?" Hack asked.

"I thought I might as well hear some music while I'm here, but that wasn't the main reason."

"Did you like it?" Hack asked him.

"To be honest," Hatfield began, then stopped.

"Go ahead," Hack told him. "Henry's not here to defend himself. He's gone."

"But he's not gone," Hatfield said.

"He's gone if I can't find him," Hack said.

"I did find him," Hatfield said. "He's living in a small town about forty miles outside Chicago."

27 Henry

Hack pulled into the Safe Retreat Nursing Home lot and parked. He got out of his Audi and walked towards the double glass doors he guessed must be the back entrance.

A blonde woman about forty was leaning against the brick wall a few yards from the doors. A green medical shift hung loose over her thin body. She held a lit cigarette to her lips. The smoke eddied up from her into the chill air. A few butts were scattered in the shallow dregs of snow around her feet.

She asked, "You here to see a resident?"

"Yes," Hack said.

"I'm Nurse Rowe." She dropped the cigarette into the snow. It sizzled. She stamped it twice. "Come on in."

Nurse Rowe opened the door and went in and stood behind a little desk. Hack followed her and stood in front of it. She flipped open a large spiral-bound book and picked up a pen and looked at Hack across the desk. "Who?"

"Henry Wadsworth," Hack said.

"Dear old Henry?" She smiled and nodded. "He was a sweet old guy."

"Was?"

Her smile faded. "I mean, he hasn't said much to anyone for a while."

"How long?"

"Maybe two years." She examined Hack more closely. "Your relationship?

Hack gambled. Maybe PC would finally work to his advantage. "I'm his son."

She looked Hack over. He beamed his most endearing smile at her, the one which charmed no one, especially women.

She ignored his effort. She leafed through the pages of her visitors' book. She said in a neutral voice, "You haven't visited him much."

"I know."

Her leafing brought her to the front of her book. "At all, I don't think."

"I've been out of the country."

"He's lived here seven years."

"It's been rough," Hack said. He hoped she wouldn't ask about birthday cards or phone calls.

She didn't. "You could have emailed him," she said. "Even after he stopped talking to us anymore, he still spent a lot of time on the Internet. Though we couldn't tell what he got out of it."

"I didn't know about that."

"We had to take away his phone and his credit card. He was always ordering things. Once they delivered a melodica to him. A little musical instrument, like a harmonica, but with keys."

"I've heard about those," Hack said.

"We had to send it back. I mean, what use could he make of it?"

"What use indeed," Hack said.

"May I see your ID?"

"Of course." He took out his wallet and showed her his driver's license.

She inspected it. She wrote the numbers down in her visitors' book. "We have to protect our patients."

"Of course," Hack said.

"Please fill out this form," she said. She laid a sheet in front of him on the desk.

He took a pen from the cup on the desk and filled out the form. He checked the "relationship" box for "son."

"Sign here," she said pointing to a line. "Here and here and here as well."

Hack signed everywhere instructed.

She removed a gray mask from the top of the stack on the desk and stretched the thin straps behind her ears and lifted the front over her face. It covered her almost up to her eyes and down over her Adam's apple. On its front the mask had a big knob with a famous brand name.

"N95," Hack thought he heard her say.

He asked, "What's that?"

"N95," she said again in a muffled voice. She handed him one. "A mask which may do some good. Our residents are old and vulnerable."

Hack took the mask and put it on like her.

Hack hated the whole mask thing. Even at peak Wuhan Covid epidemic, Ojibwa City merchants had never enforced mask mandates, unless a bureaucrat from the government happened to be snooping around inside.

She said, "When I think about it, I guess I can understand why you never phoned Henry. Like I told you, he doesn't speak. So please don't expect too much."

Nurse Rowe led Hack into the building and through a labyrinth of narrow hallways. Stark white illumination turned every detail of the place clear and obvious.

Safe Retreat management had painted the walls in sassy yellow and insolent orange and had hung bright nature paintings and gold cardboard daisies everywhere. It was like visiting Sarai's old kindergarten.

Names in cheerful red cursive hung on every door they passed: "The Gundersons"; "The Smiths"; "Ralph".

Just past "Molly," they arrived at a half-open door for "Henry." Nurse Rowe said, "Here we are."

She pushed the door open. Just inside the room door was another door on the right. Must lead to a bathroom. Past that door was the room itself. There was a made-up single bed next to the beige wall. There was a single black chair in front of an empty desk. No photos of anyone anywhere.

His back to Hack and Nurse Rowe, a man sat in a wheelchair by a window to the outside, looking through it. On the other side of the window, a pair of blue jays hopped around in the piled-up snow.

The man turned his head and stared at Hack and Nurse Rowe through glasses thick as the front lenses of binoculars. His wide black frames spanned and nearly covered his slack face.

He wore a blue Chicago Bears sweatshirt a world too long and wide, reaching down from his thin shoulders and spreading across the thighs of his blue sweatpants.

Even sitting, his frame was bent and spare. His once thick muscles—if it was Hack's Henry—had shrunk away. The tendons which underlay his cheeks had atrophied, and the loose brown skin of his face sagged. Patches of unshaven white whiskers flecked his chin and neck. His nose was bigger than Hack remembered.

Was this the right man?

The man glared with suspicion at Hack and Nurse Rowe.

"I'm sorry," Nurse Rowe said from behind Hack. "You see?"

For a moment nobody spoke.

His expression did not change, but the man spoke. "Nate," Henry said. "Take that damned rag off your face." It was the same baritone, warm and authoritative, incongruous from this enfeebled presence.

"Well," Nurse Rowe murmured from behind Hack. "I guess I called that wrong. Visiting ends at four. You've got an hour and a half."

She disappeared. The two men were alone.

"Henry," Hack said.

"Please take that thing off," Henry said, "And sit."

Hack yanked off the mask and dropped it on the floor. He grabbed up the black desk chair and set it down a few feet from Henry and settled his rear end on its hard edge.

The two inspected each other awhile.

Henry asked, "You here for a session?"

"Sure," Hack said.

For now, Hack kept the envelope with the $300 cash in his pocket.

"Good," Henry said. "There are a few things I never got around to mentioning."

"Like what?"

"Like about Debussy, for example."

"I thought you told me all about Debussy."

"Not everything," Henry said. "There's always more to say about Debussy."

The End